CW01669870

v|b|z ZAGREB

istrosbooks

NA MARGINI
ON THE MARGINS

BOOK SERIES
NA MARGINI / ON THE MARGINS

book no. 22

EDITOR-IN-CHIEF:
Drago Glamuzina

MANAGING EDITOR:
Sandra Ukalović

Lada Vukić
Special Needs

PUBLISHER:
V.B.Z. d.o.o., Zagreb
10010 Zagreb, Dračevička 12
tel.: 01/6235-419, fa: 01/6235-418
e-mail: info@vbz.hr
www.vbz.hr

FOR CO-PUBLISHER:
Istros Books
Conway Hall, 25 Red Lion Square,
London, WC1R 4RL
e-mail: info@istrosbooks.com

FOR PUBLISHER:
Mladen Zatezalo

EDITOR:
Susan Curtis

PROOFREADER:
Morelle Smith

LAYOUT:
V.B.Z. studio, Zagreb

PRINTED IN:
Znanje d.o.o., Zagreb
August 2021

This project has been funded with support from the European Commission.
This publication reflects the views only of the author, and the Commission cannot be held responsible for any use which may be made of the information contained therein.

Lada Vukić
Special Needs

Translated by
Christina Pribichevich-Zorić

v|b|z ZAGREB
2021

NA MARGINI
ON THE MARGINS

BOOK SERIES
NA MARGINI / ON THE MARGINS

book no. 22

ORIGINAL TITLE
Lada Vukić
Specijalna potreba

The publication of this book is supported by a grant from the Ministry of Culture and Media of the Republic of Croatia.

Republic
of Croatia
Ministry
of Culture
and Media
Republika
Hrvatska
Ministarstvo
kulture
i medija

ISBN-13: 978-1-912545-91-9

Contents

This is a work of fiction.
Any resemblance to actual persons
is coincidental and unintentional

RUBBISH

MY NAME is Emil and I'm ten years old. The same as the number of fingers I have when I count them one by one, hiding my hands under my school desk and counting. I don't know what will happen when I reach eleven. I don't mean fingers, I mean eleven years of age. How will I count then? The teacher says that fingers have nothing to do with counting. You think with your head, not with your fingers. But that's the only way I know how to count. I do know how to describe the number eleven, though. It's two ones standing next to each other. Like two of Emil's drooping heads. Like most of my low scores in assessment.

I don't go to school on Saturdays, so I have lots of time to do my exercises. They're not body-building exercises, they'll never help me build up a mass of muscles, I'm pretty sure of that. I've been doing them for a long time now, but nothing has changed. My tops and trousers still hang on me. Mum calls them exercises in social skills. At first, I did them in my slippers; in soft, warm, noiseless slippers with sticky straps. I would spend ages playing with those straps. In fact, I still do. Fastening and unfastening them makes a terrific sound, like when you crush dry leaves with your fingers. I do it until the sticky part wears out and stops making that sound. It always makes mum mad. Not because the sound is gone, but because the slippers are ruined.

Some time ago she forbade me from wearing them when I do my exercises on Saturdays. I wear shoes now, but she refuses to help me with them the way she used to. She says I have to do it myself, without anybody's help. It's for my own good. So it takes time for me to put them on and tie the laces. The latest pair doesn't have a sticky strap, just plain soundless shoelaces. It sometimes takes a long time for me to tie them into a decent bow. Usually, I fail, so it's good that in the end mum says: "Never mind, you'll do better the next time. Nobody was born particularly bright or particularly able. Everything in life, Emil, is a matter of training and practice. You just have to practice more than others."

On Saturdays, apart from putting on my shoes, I also practice taking out the rubbish. And I've started practising going to the kiosk to buy the newspaper, lollipops, matches…That's also called exercising the brain. I'm ten years old, so when will I do it if not now. Mum gives me the money, tells me how much it costs, and then I try to guess how much change the lady at the kiosk has to give me back. I'm usually wrong because there's no guessing when it comes to maths. You have to be good at working it out.

Today I managed to tie my shoelaces on the first go. My hands didn't cramp, not once.

"Well done, Emil! See how you can do anything if you try?!" Mum said, happily looking up from the piece of fabric she was cutting with her scissors. She beckoned me over, brushed my hair back with her hand and kissed me on the forehead.

I take the big rubbish bag and head for the door to take down in the lift. I hear her say not to forget to stop off at the professor's on the first floor.

"Pick up his rubbish as well. Last Saturday you forgot."

Naturally. That happens to me a lot. I start off with one thing and finish with another.

Like the Saturday when there was an empty slipper box in front of his door, next to the rubbish bag. I collect shoe, slipper and trainer boxes. Although mum always says that it would be better if I collected something else, something that other children collect. Because who collects shoeboxes? Where did I ever see such a thing, she asks. It's silly to collect old cardboard boxes. What's wrong with stamps or picture cards?

Well, nothing. But stamps and picture cards don't have that smell of leather and rubber that lingers in cardboard boxes for a long time, and they don't have the picture of the shoes on the outside of the box. When I see the picture, I know right away what's inside. I know where you can go with them. That day, I took the professor's box straight home and put it at the back of my wardrobe with the others. Later, when I went back down again, I forgot all about his rubbish.

The hallway is quiet as I walk to the lift. Too quiet. There's only the sound of my shoes, the ones I don't like. Not because it's hard to tie the shoelaces, but…

You can't buy my shoes in a shop. They're not displayed in the shop window like other shoes. And they don't have the logo of a famous brand. I get them from Uncle Mario. So, no Nikes, no Adidas, just - Uncle Mario. And who wants shoes called *Uncle Mario*? I mean, nobody normal. And I'm normal, though sometimes they say I'm not. First, he makes imprints of my feet, which are then used to make the shoes. I've seen that he does the same with others, so I'm not the only one. There are others like me, with special feet. But that doesn't mean anything to me because I don't like being special, I want to be ordinary. I wish my feet were ordinary, and that I could choose the shoes I want from the shop window. I've got nothing against Uncle Mario, but he already knows that he mustn't ever touch my feet to make a clearer imprint. Mum does that. The last time she said right in front of him that I was childish and too big to be so silly. How long did I plan to keep this up? I don't know, I just know that it has nothing to do with how old I am. We tried a hundred times and I simply couldn't get it right. It's not as easy as tying shoelaces or taking out the rubbish.

When the shoes are made, I try them out in front of the mirror in his clinic. We watch how I walk in my new, special shoes. To them they look great. But to me?

Mum checks if my new shoes are better and more comfortable than the old pair. I don't tell her that they are just as loud and heavy and ugly as all the previous pairs. Until I wear them in, they make even more noise than the old ones. All my shoes have one thing in common: they attract attention. Most people look at them and then quickly turn away. As if they hadn't noticed anything. Kids stare and sometimes turn around to take a second look. As if they hadn't seen enough. I know that because I turn around too, to see who will outlast the other. I'm good at rubbernecking. I mostly win.

The wind isn't howling through the broken windows in the hallway today. Sometimes I think about it. About the wind. How it hurls at the holes in the windowpanes. I wonder if it gets hurt by the shards of glass sticking out of the window frames. Why else would it moan like that? The glass is always missing in our hallway windows. It's there for a while and then – *bang!* You can hear footsteps running away and laughter. One thing is for sure – I have nothing to do with it! I didn't have anything to do with it last year either, when Mr. Franjo from the tenth floor accused me. Mum kept trying to assure him: "Can't you see?! I'd be only too happy if he'd broken the window! Happy! I'd pay for the damages and be the happiest woman in the world!" Mr. Franjo said that this was the last time the money for a new window was coming out of the cash reserve. The next time, we'd all have to think about what to do. Leave it broken so that everybody can see what kind of people live in this building! We're not spending our common funds on badly raised children. Is that clear?!

It was perfectly clear to me, except: what's a broken window got to do with mum's happiness?

Clomp-clomp – all you can hear are my shoes as I get out on the first floor and leave my rubbish bag in the lift. I always do that because it's stupid to carry my own rubbish bag just to pick up another. It's better if nobody sees me. Professor Antun left his rubbish in front of his door and I took it as we'd agreed.

"Nobody understands better than me what it's like to have someone with a disability in the house. You don't have to tell me, dear professor. Of course, either Emil or I will pick up your rubbish and take it out to the wheelie bin. Don't worry."

The two of them came to an agreement, and that's how it started. Sometimes she did it, sometimes I did it.

As I was heading for the lift, its inner iron door closed shut like the jaws of an animal. It rumbled up, taking my rubbish with it.

Well, I didn't feel like waiting for it to come back down. It's hard to explain to others that I didn't forget it and I didn't get off on the first floor by mistake. I'm not muddled and I didn't get out on the first floor by mistake. I know that G means ground floor. I'm not so crazy as to admit that I pick up the professor's rubbish, in case somebody else got the same idea. And where would that leave me? This exercise was getting on my nerves. But I didn't tell anybody. Not mum and not the professor. That's what happens when you love somebody; you don't talk about not liking the things you have to do. It's only one flight of stairs down to the ground floor and I'd made up my mind: in addition to tying my shoelaces and taking out the rubbish, I'm going to practice walking down the stairs.

Holding on to the railing, I carefully walked down. My shoes clomped as if made to be both heard and seen. Once, the noise caused a misunderstanding. I still think it was nothing more than that. A woman living in our apartment block, the one who receives the magazine *It's Good to Do Good* in her letterbox, said: "Can you be a bit quieter, Emil? I was just taking my nap! Why are you going back and forth in front of my door like that? You're making a racket!" I looked at her and shook my head, because sadly I couldn't walk any quieter, not unless I took off my shoes and walked in my bare feel. Mum went crazy when I told her about it. I tried to tell her that maybe I'd misheard, but that made her even angrier:

"Emil, we both know that you couldn't have misheard! You can misunderstand but not mishear!"

And that was that. End of story. Ever since, the two of them pretend not to see or hear each other. Even though we live side by side. Door to door. Wall to wall.

Luckily, it didn't take long to go down the stairs. I quickly found myself on the spacious ground floor. I stopped at the letterbox and put down the rubbish bag. I climbed onto the old chair that had been standing under the letterboxes for ages. OK, mum says it's not nice to poke your nose into other people's business because then you can expect them to do the same thing to you. And nobody likes a nosy parker. But I couldn't help it and, anyway, I was bored. Our letterbox was empty and of no interest. So, I peered into the others. Some had fashion catalogues, others had letters and postcards. Miss Vjeka had received the latest issue of the magazine *It's Good to Do Good*. The professor's letterbox was crammed with unpaid bills. Lying on the floor were leaflets from the Supernova shopping centre. I saw a great pair of trainers on the front, the kind I wanted for my next birthday! I could wear them at least on Saturdays and Sundays, even if I had to wear my special shoes to school. I decided to tell mum when I got back upstairs and I shoved the leaflet into my pocket. I had just picked up the professor's rubbish bag when a strange, unusual person came bursting in.

He ran in as if somebody was chasing him. The police, maybe. You know, like in the movies. He slammed shut the door, crouched down and peered out the window. So, I was right, he was hiding from somebody. He hadn't noticed me because he was all worked up and I was quiet and frozen to the spot. His heart was thudding like a rolling stone. I heard it without even trying. It's always been like that with me. I went completely still. I barely breathed, hoping he wouldn't notice me, that maybe he'd leave the way he came, when the danger outside passed.

In the end, it was my feet that gave me away. My legs had gone stiff from standing still for so long, I had to move. And it's impossible not to hear my shoes.

"Hey?...What? Who are you? What are you doing here?" he said, jumping up as if stung. He surprised me. What kind of question was that: who am I? Nobody had ever asked me that before. And I get asked all sorts of questions…

I didn't say anything. First of all, I didn't know what to say. Secondly, that's what happens to me with people. My mouth won't open. I said to myself: *I'm me and I'm not doing anything*, but, naturally, nobody could hear it. So, it turned out that I didn't say anything.

"What are you doing here, I said!" In two bounds he was right next to me, peering into my face. Then he decided to resort to his hands, probably because I still wasn't saying anything! Luckily, at the last minute, his hands froze, suspended in the air by the sight of my shoes. I could see him examining them, not knowing what to do with his hands anymore. He fell silent for a minute, maybe thinking it over before saying:

"Helloooo?! Can't you talk, kid? Why have you gone all stiff like that? You live here? So, you were going to take out your garbage, huh?"

I shook my head, clutching the professor's rubbish bag even tighter.

"What, then?!"

"It's…not…my…rubbish."

"Whose is it?"

I didn't answer. I wondered why the two of us were talking at all. And why was it about the rubbish?

"What's the matter with you, kid? Are you normal?"

He put his index finger on his forehead to show me what he thought about my brain. I know what it means when somebody looks you in the eye and twirls his finger on his forehead!

Sometimes they do that to me at school and even say: Emil-Imbecile!

"Agree…ment."

"What agreement? What are you talking about? What are you, some kind of dustman?"

Just then, a lady mum and I call *It's Good to Do Good* appeared. We were so wrapped up in questions and answers that we didn't hear her. Even I didn't hear her! She stepped out of the lift, blocked the door with her shopping cart and just stood there staring at us. I saw that my rubbish bag was where I had left it. She said "Good Morning" to me. And then she said it again. I didn't say anything, I just continued to gaze down at my shoes and at the ceramic tiles underfoot. The man was facing the letterboxes and pretended not to see *It's Good to Do Good.* Saying hello wasn't in his veins, as my mother would say. He pretended to be looking for something, but naturally he wasn't looking for anybody. He ran his eyes over the unfamiliar names.

"I said Good Morning, Emil!", she said, enunciating each word clearly for the third time. I looked at her and said to myself, *Good Morning.* Nobody heard it. Instead of looking at me, squinting her eyes she examined the unknown man's leather motorcycle jacket. Finally, she mumbled, "nice company and well brought up." She took hold of her shopping cart, opened the front door and left.

Time was short. I had to get the rubbish bag out of the lift before it went up to another floor again. As I was about to move, he shouted:

"Heeeey. Slow down! Who said you could move! Stay put!"

All I needed was for my rubbish bag to get away from me again. I'd taken only a step or two when I felt his hand on my shoulder. I screamed so loudly that you could hear it on the top floor! Or I simply thought you could hear it and that somebody would come and help me: mum, the professor, anybody! I don't know, maybe my scream shocked him too because he let me go and said:

"C'mon, shut up!"

He said that if I didn't shut up, he'd make me! With his hands!

"You decide. It's up to you!"

I chose to shut up but pointed at the lift:

"The rub...bish."

We walked towards the lift together. Me facing forward and he looking back at the front door of the building. Was that somebody about to burst in and nab him? Well, let them, I thought, then I'll be able to throw that stupid rubbish into the wheelie bin! But nobody came, not even when the man used his foot to keep the lift door open. Not even when I picked the other rubbish bag up off the floor. He kept his eye on me as if I could run away in these shoes. I couldn't! I couldn't get anywhere in these shoes! You can count on it!

"What's this shit with the rubbish bags? Huh? One takes the lift and you carry the other?" For a second, I thought he would tell me again that I'm not normal or just point at his forehead. But no. Suddenly he said something that completely floored me:

"You know what, kid, let me ask you something. I know we didn't get off on the right foot, but I hope you won't rat on me."

"!?!"

"Yep. I need a little help. I can see that you're really a good kid, and here I am sounding off like an idiot. Don't worry. Everything is OK. I'm just a little mistrustful of people I don't know. Like I said, I need your help…"

He bent down and now we were at eye level. It gave him a chance, I guess, to smile at me. That's how I saw that he was missing a tooth, which meant that he was like me, he didn't like dentists. That's something mum can't help me with. She says she can't take a drill and fix my teeth. It's not at all like helping to make an imprint of my foot. It's more complicated.

"Whaddya say?"

First, I thought of shaking my head no. But then it occurred to me that I could wind up missing a tooth of my own. Second, I can't explain why, but even after everything, I liked the attention I was getting. Nobody had ever asked me for a favour before. Not ever! It was always others helping me. My religion teacher says that the hand that gives is more blessed than the hand that receives. I'm sure that means something good. Maybe this, what was happening now, was like that: a blessed hand.

I nodded. It was better to make peace. We looked as if we were mad at each other, though I don't know how we got there.

He told me to imagine that the two of us were playing a kind of hide-and-seek, where he gave me an imaginary object and I had to hide it somewhere. Somewhere around the building. Where would I hide it?

I had to think fast and I'm not known for being a fast thinker. I'm ten years old and I'm not very good at school. I was afraid to say that I didn't know where. They'd never let me play hide-and-seek at school because I can't run. But I know how it's played. You run and hide. So you have to have fast feet and a great hiding place. He seemed to sense my problem, so he suggested that I stay put and just tell him where. I thought of Auntie Lilia. She helps me do tests to improve my learning, my memory and all that. When mum asks her how I'm doing, she says: "We'll know that, Miss Marina, when Emil finds himself in a new, unfamiliar situation."

Maybe this was just such a situation. Nothing like this had ever happened to me before. I said to myself: *Emil, think, open your mouth and speak, speak...*

"The rubbish"

"The rubbish? No way! You have to return the object. You understand?"

No! How could I return it? From where? From my mind? I thought that we were imagining this game. Imagining the object. That nothing was for real. I looked at my feet. The packet, actually the five soft white packets he'd taken out of the pocket of his motorcycle jacket would easily fit into my ugly high shoes.

"Cool!", he said enthusiastically to my new proposal. "Listen, go and throw out those...rubbish bags. And not a word to anybody. Not about me...not about that," he said, pointing at my shoes. "Not a peep or I'll wring your neck! You get it? This is now our little secret. You be here in the hallway tomorrow at ten! To return those. Now, beat it! And...be careful!"

He pressed the button for floor 10 and the lift door closed behind him.

I went outside to the wheelie bin with my hands full and my shoes full. And almost my pants full.

It's Good to Do Good

IT RAINED all day the next day, even though at first it had looked as if it would snow. That happens to me too. Things start off looking one way and wind up looking another. I'd just finished doing my homework. I'd made butterflies out of modelling clay for my nature and social studies class. The subject was "Winter and Snow". Modelling clay is good for exercising my fingers and I really like to work with it. I'd just finished when somebody rang at the door.

Mum lifted her foot off the pedal of the sewing machine and I put my third butterfly down on the table. We looked at each other and thought: Who could that be? Then it dawned on me: the man with the missing tooth from the day before. He'd come upstairs to punish me because I hadn't shown up downstairs this morning! He had come to wring my neck. That's what he'd said: "Don't say a word or else..." While mum went to the door, I rushed to my room to get my piggybank. I'd decided that I would give it to him at the door and say: "Don't worry! It's all there inside!" The piggybank had no money in it anyway, just his packets. I had to find a way to tell him that I hadn't taken the rubbish out today or gone to the kiosk. It was raining and I never go out if it's slippery. Mum won't let me.

But when she opened the door, it was *It's Good to Do Good* standing there, which was only a tiny bit better than if it had been the man with the missing tooth. Anyway, we call Miss Vjeka that because it suits her better. Mum always raises her hands and makes a *click-click* sound with her two fingers. I didn't understand why she did that, so she tried to explain.

"Emil, can you imagine that woman doing anything good for anybody?"

"No. But why do we call her that if she isn't good?"

"Hmmm...I don't know how to explain it to you...it's a caricature."

"Cari...what?"

It sounded like caries, like when you've got a cavity, but I'm sure it had nothing to do with that. *It's Good to Do Good* had perfect teeth. She smiled a lot while saying bad things. "It's called a phony smile," mum said.

"How come you don't understand her nickname and that it's the opposite of what she's like?" mum kept trying to explain.

I didn't understand, full stop. But we kept on calling her that because we simply got used to it. The same thing happened in my class, everybody just got used to calling me: Emil-imbecile.

It's Good to Do Good had size 40 slippers on her feet. I know that because the box her slippers came in is at the back of my wardrobe. Mum doesn't know about it, naturally, because I'm sure she'd make me throw it away. First of all, because the two of them don't greet each other anymore, and secondly, because mum says that those big feet walk over whatever they encounter! Once she even said the word – corpses! That's hard to believe, but I know that mum usually exaggerates when she's angry. Anyway, everybody knows that corpses are in cemeteries. Under the ground. So how can she walk over what's already been walked over? It's like leaves; when they turn brown, they fall off the tree and disappear. The earth absorbs them. That's the end of it.

It's Good to Do Good was wearing a flowery housedress, her hair piled up like the bird's nest under our window. It goes without saying that mum was dumbstruck when she saw her. She was so surprised that for a second her chest fell silent and she was speechless.

It's Good to Do Good took advantage of that second of silence to ask mum if she could come in because she had something important to tell her. It was better if nobody overheard it. She was perfectly aware that mum wasn't talking to her, but she hadn't meant anything bad when what happened between them happened and she had said what she'd said, especially not when it concerned a disabled child, because she knew what that was like.

"And what is that like?" mum asked, raising her voice, folding her arms across her chest, and her heart, which had stopped, but was now beating faster than usual. "Do you have a disabled child at home too?" she said, though she knew full well that *It's Good to Do Good* didn't. That she was alone and had no children. Unless you count her two old orange cats which, to be fair, she does sometimes call her children, but...mum says it's not normal not to know how to draw a line between people and animals and to call animals children, and children animals...

"Well...," *It's Good to Do Good* started. "I didn't come here for that reason, Marina, I didn't come to argue. I came to tell you that I'm not the heartless person you think I am, I am a decent person who doesn't like conflicts and when I see something that's wrong I have to say something, or else

I'd have a guilty conscience and it would be hypocritical of me to ever step foot in church again, and you know that I am a pious woman, which means that, come hell or high water, I have to tell you what I've come to say."

That was a long sentence and *It's Good to Do Good* said it in one breath. In one go. Without stammering.

I looked down. The new pair of slippers she'd brought back from her last trip were more interesting than what they were saying at the door. Not trip, pilgrimage. She always told people that she went on pilgrimages, not on meaningless, aimless trips. Printed on the slippers were words, messages about…walking and travelling. My religion teacher sometimes talks like that. Like the messages on these slippers. They said: "There is only one path to…," the last word trailed off onto the other side of her left little toe. Or: "… shall pave the way to You", the beginning hiding behind the heel. But you could clearly read "Teach me the art of small steps" on the front of the right slipper. Whoever wrote those words had never seen my feet! I don't know who would want to walk and never get to where they were going.

Mum did not take her eyes off her face. Mystified, she opened wide the door. She pointed to the kitchen and even asked if she wanted a cup of coffee. She sent me to my room, telling me to get back to my homework. She forgot that I'd finished it and shown her the butterflies that were due the next day. She'd even asked me over her shoulder why on earth I had my piggybank in my hand. Where was I taking it?

I didn't say anything. There was nothing to say unless I lied. And I wasn't good at that. At lying. At inventing.

It's Good to Do Good didn't want any coffee and didn't want to sit down, she remained standing there like a pillar. Then, raising a finger, she bared her teeth:

"You know, Marina, your boy is going to be a problem!"

"What do you mean, Vjeka? What kind of problem? Don't I have enough problems as it is?"

"It seems not. You see, yesterday..." and she coughed, cleared her throat and wriggled her toes in her slippers, "Firstly, let me say that I know your boy takes out the rubbish on Saturdays, but he left it in the lift. And not for the first time! I didn't say anything before, but I finally said to myself, Vjeka, it's wrong to keep quiet, you have to say something! So here it is, Marina: why do you give him chores that he can't do? Secondly, he doesn't greet me, even when I say hello first, and repeat it, though the proper thing would be for a younger person to greet an older person first. That's the first rule of good manners. To greet your neighbours. To be polite. We are all capable of that..."

"What on earth are you talking about? You've come here to take me to task over a greeting? I was naïve to think that you'd finally come to your senses! Go, get out of here!", mum exploded. "I thought you were going to tell me who knows what, but it turns out it's one nonsense after another. You know where the door is. Leave, this minute! My child suffers from mutism! Along with the basic diagnosis, it's visible to the naked eye! Do you know what mutism is or don't you?"

"Never heard of it, but I know that Emil isn't tongue-tied, if the word can apply to speech. He was speaking perfectly well with that dealer downstairs yesterday. I heard him with my own ears. Though, let's be clear, they both played dumb when they saw me, pretending not to know each other. But I can smell a criminal and good-for-nothing from miles away. And you would, too, Marina, if you volunteered like me for the Association for Combatting Drug Addiction Among the Young. It's my fifth year with them now. So, I know that environment very well. Better than very well! Your boy could be vulnerable because he's naïve, and wouldn't cope, and the next thing you know, he'll be up to his neck in addiction. Even children from good families fall prey, not to mention others. They start out of curiosity…"

"What's the matter with you? Are *you* on some kind of drug? What are you talking about? What dealer? You are a sad, lonely, sensation-seeking woman looking for attention! I'm not going to say you're crazy because only a psychiatrist can give you the proper diagnosis. Now, get out of here!!! How many times do I have to say it?! Ouuut!", mum yelled. Meanwhile the piggybank was sweating in my hand. My whole body was trembling, and my eyes were blinking nervously. It looked as if I was lying even though I hadn't said a word.

"I knew it!", *It's Good to Do Good* said. Walking backwards in her silent messaged slippers. "You parents are all the same. The first thing you do is leap to the defence of your child rather than believe an adult, even though I have no reason to hate or dislike your child. I'm simply pointing out faults in his upbringing, although I do understand that it may be partly due to the absence of a father. Anyway, that's what I came to say. And if I see that dealer hanging around downstairs again and your son talking to him…"

"My son doesn't talk to people he doesn't know!" said mum through her teeth, clenching her fists and jutting out her jaw. My piggybank kept treacherously slipping from my hands. I couldn't move. As if my feet were glued to the floor. Meanwhile, I was holding a secret in my hands that I had promised to keep.

"If I see him one more time..."

"What will you do if you see him, Vjeka? Say that your mission is to do good?"

"Well, one could say that. But, yes, I will call social services, Marina. That's what I came to tell you. They can investigate your case and check your fitness as a single parent."

Boy, did our front door slam with a bang! Like a firecracker on New Year's Eve. Flakes of plaster even fell off the wall. My Smurf next to the phone rocked on its heels and toppled over onto its back. I thought the same thing would happen to me, but my legs remained locked at my knees like two pieces of wood. I was still clutching my piggybank, thinking: what does "dealer" mean? And social services? And what am I going to tell mum if she asks if what *It's Good to Do Good* said is true?

Maybe I should start practicing lying. The way other people do. They lie and nothing happens. For example, everybody in class knows that Tonko lies when he talks and when he writes. He lies more than Pinocchio. But everybody thinks he's fun and amusing. Especially when he reads aloud his essays on going to Mars or going on safari in Africa. That's what they call killing elephants and rhinos. I like animals. If a safari was called "Death in Africa" I bet they'd find it a little less amusing. The teacher always pats him on the head and says: "What an imagination you have!" She never says: "What lies you tell!" Tonko is already saying that he will write comic strips when he grows up. As for me, I don't know yet. Probably because I'm not growing very much. I think that's my problem. It's my shoes and legs. That's why I'll always be small, puny, with no imagination. Professor Antun says the same thing. He says it's a pity about my special hearing. I could achieve all sorts of things if it weren't for my….other problems. Whichever way you look at it, nothing is right.

When we were alone again, mum went to the kitchen. The glass in her hand was trembling as she filled it with water. She seemed to have forgotten all about me. As if what happened was because of Miss Vjeka, not me. I heard her open the top kitchen cabinet, take out a little cardboard packet, and press down on the foil, making a pill pop out. She had a long drink of water. I went to my room, but my hands were still cold and sweaty. I put the piggybank on the desk and thought: what now? Should I go back to the kitchen and ask her what she thinks about my butterflies? Or ask her what she thinks about the strange message printed on Miss Vjeka's slippers?

I took a few steps towards the kitchen door. The noise in her chest stopped me in my tracks. It was like that movie when lots of broken-down clocks in the watch-maker's shop start working at the same time. Both the alarm clocks and the cuckoo clocks!

I figured it wasn't the right moment to ask my question, so I went back to my room, sat on my bed and took off my slippers.

The sound of rustling dry leaves filled the space.

Butterflies

THE TEACHER said that the butterflies were no good. I didn't understand why not, since they'd arrived in the classroom in one piece and undamaged. Some of the children were surprised by them, others laughed. There were more of these others, who always laughed at whatever I made or said. As usual, I didn't understand a thing because I'm never sure about funny things. How they should look or be heard. For example, I never know exactly when to laugh. Sometimes I try to guess, but I start either too soon or too late. So, I always wait for the others to laugh first, before joining in.

Everybody, I mean everybody, reacts by saying: "Look at the imbecile stupidly laughing! Admit it, again you didn't understand anything!"

I shake my head, because naturally I didn't understand, I was simply trying to guess, and everybody found that even funnier. Again, I'm never sure what they find funny: that I don't get it or that I admit that I don't get it. Mum says that first I have to understand the joke and then the laughter will come of itself. It's no good pretending to be cleverer than you are because in the end you can turn out looking even stupider. You have to be who you are in life, full stop. You have to know in your head exactly how to subtract the serious from the unserious. What's left is funny. Naturally. Like in maths. That's why I get it wrong.

"Can anybody hear what you hear?" mum says when she wants to comfort me.

I shake my head because I've never met anybody like me.

"You see, we don't all have the same abilities, and you certainly can do something that others can only dream of. Don't worry about laughter and jokes at your expense; every fool has his own kind of fun."

The teacher didn't have a single good thing to say about the butterflies. She said that as usual I hadn't been listening when she was assigning the homework. That I was incapable of listening properly to even the simplest thing. I tried to say something in my defence, especially regarding my hearing and listening, but I had trouble with the words. My mouth stayed shut, full stop.

"C'mon, tell me what've they got to do with anything?" she insisted, frowning with disapproval. "It's about to snow outside, and you bring butterflies. Where can we see butterflies in the winter, Emil?"

Nowhere, I said to myself and thought of Tonko. If I were Tonko maybe she would praise me. Maybe she would say: "What an imagination!" Maybe it's just me who sees imagination in my pieces.

"I heard…"

"What? Butterflies?"

"Snow."

"Snow?"

As soon as I said it, everyone from the first row to the last burst out laughing. It spread like waves in the sea. I didn't laugh, of course, because I didn't find anything funny about it. Especially not when they shouted from the back row: "Look at the imbecile lie!"

"Alright! Quiet, children!" the teacher said, clapping her hands to silence them. "Let's say you did hear it. Then why didn't you use the modelling clay to make snowflakes, like Natalia, or a frozen lake or whatever, so that we know winter has arrived. Butterflies come with the spring. How many times do I have to keep repeating these things to you? The most I can give you for your incorrectly done homework is a grade 2, and even that's a stretch. You exhaust me, Emil. It's a shame, because you could have achieved a higher grade on such an easy assignment. I don't know what to do with you. This isn't maths, and I'm not asking you how much is two plus two."

Just as well. I struggle with maths. OK, I struggle with other subjects too, but especially with maths. It's my hardest subject at school. I always practice it at home with mum. We start with apples: "Emil, you have two apples and I give you two more, how many apples do you have now?" I look at them, all nice and red, mum calls them Johnathins (though they're not thin at all!), she bought them to make me an apple pie, and I say: "Four."

"Good! So what's two plus two then?" she says, removing the apples from the table.

"???"

I can't stop wondering where the apples she just mentioned have gone. Why are only the numbers left? What's the number? What am I adding? Why am I adding? Mum says that I'm bad at abstract thought.

"Emil, think with your head, not with your hands," the teacher always says when she catches me using my fingers under my desk to add and subtract.

How am I supposed to do that? When you count, your fingers are on your hands, not in your head!

"There's always some problem with you, Emil," she says when we're alone in the classroom and she doesn't want anybody to hear what she has to say to me. "A special school would be best for your development. You're not keeping up with the programme here, and I don't have time to work with you individually. I don't know what to do, this is becoming impossible for both of us..."

The best thing to do is nothing. That's the answer I always want to give. Because the hands and feet problem is mine, not hers. So, I don't understand why she's mentioning a special school. Because I'm not special, I'm ordinary. As ordinary as ordinary can be!!! Natalia is the one who is special, in every way. She's specially pretty and especially good. And she specially invited me to her birthday party on a hand-made card. She's the only one in the whole class who ever invited me. I couldn't believe it when it happened last year. I heard some of the children whisper to her: "Did your mother make you invite him?" And I also heard: "I'm not coming if you invite that imbecile. Your choice!"

I didn't go to the party. Not because of the word *imbecile,* but because I didn't want to go without mum. And mum didn't want to go because grown-ups don't go to children's birthday parties. Full stop.

"You're ten years old, Emil!" she said. "It's time for you to socialize. It's for your own good."

Natalia didn't celebrate her birthday this year. Or else she did, but she forgot to invite me. Or else she didn't forget, but she didn't dare invite me because of her friends. Or else there was another reason, but I don't know what. I didn't ask.

But I did wonder why the teacher never mentioned a special school for Tonko. He stood shoulder to shoulder with me when it came to bad grades. Shoulder to shoulder. Plus, he got into fights and swore. In that respect he was top of the class. The only thing he was good at was writing and drawing cartoons. The teacher praised his imagination, but she didn't forget to tell him that being talented was not enough. It was important to read. Writing and reading went hand in hand, just as swearing and fighting went with something that had nothing to do with either culture or literature.

But back to the butterflies.

She'd just opened the gradebook, when Nikola, the new PE teacher walked into the classroom. That same second, she lost her train of thought and immediately forgot what she had wanted to do, although she was still holding the ballpoint pen in her hand and the ledger was open on my page. She closed the book and opened her mouth. That's to say, it broke into a smile.

It was only natural, who wouldn't gape at Professor Nikola, at all those muscles under his tight-fitting, clinging top. And then they began to whisper. I waited politely for them to stop. Meanwhile, I was thinking of some easy, quick way to ask him how you get such a muscular body. I wanted one too! I knew that you needed trainers on your feet for your muscles to develop. Nothing special could happen to your body while wearing *Uncle Mario* shoes. Everybody knew that. Professor Nikola wore trainers. I looked down from my school bench to see what brand they were and to check him out again from head to foot. I was absorbed in my thoughts when the teacher made a sound. Her cheeks were flushed. Was she sick? My mind was still on trainers and muscles, but my thoughts were disturbed by the noise coming from her chest. Professor Nikola turned to me and said:

"Emil, first I want to know what you think about what I want to propose. Would you like to join us in PE class?

Would you like to exercise? Play ball? Shoot baskets, things like that? Nothing difficult or tiring. I think physical activity would be good for you."

I was shocked by his proposal! Sometimes I dream about incredible things, mostly that I'm running and doing things I don't ordinarily do. That I'm running fast, that I'm the fastest in my class, that I'm skipping two and three steps at a time…

"Yeeess…" I heard my voice say as if it weren't mine, having said *yes, yes, yes* to myself.

"Well, well! So, we can talk when it's about something we like? Is that it, Emil? The cat gave you your tongue back, did it?" my teacher cut in, somewhat spoiling my excitement.

"Gordana, leave him alone. What child doesn't like PE? It's certainly not the thought of numbers that make us smile. Isn't that right, Emil?" Professor Nikola said in my defence.

"Ahaa…" I said, beside myself with happiness. I felt as if I were floating above my desk. Maybe I'll get a pair of trainers, I immediately thought. Trainers for PE! Finally, there was somebody here who understood me.

"Listen, Nikola" said my teacher, but she said it in a strange way. It was like when mum says to me "*listen,* Emil." But it definitely couldn't be the same. She even took him by the elbow, the sound in her chest even louder than before. "If his mother signs her approval for Emil to exercise under your supervision, then fine. I've got nothing against it and don't get me wrong. It's just that we have to be very careful, these things aren't as simple as you imagine. Think it over: do you need a burden like that? What if something happens? Who will be blamed? Who will be responsible?" she said, all the while smiling, twisting a lock of hair around her finger, even though what she was saying wasn't funny at all. I mean, it wasn't funny to me. Of course, it could be that it was funny, though why I didn't know. Because I wasn't good at adding and subtracting the serious from the unserious. That's why.

What was going on inside her didn't stop. It became louder and faster, like a train without brakes. Like in a movie I once saw. The train speeded up, but the brakes weren't working. I thought something like that was going to happen now. A disaster and explosion, like in the movie! That my teacher would burst into a thousand pieces!

"Miss..." I called out to her.

At first, she didn't hear me because she was...wrapped up in her own movie. That's what you say when you're only physically present and your mind is somewhere else. But her movie had nothing to do with the movies we see on TV. It was just something you said. She taught me that because she often says: "Emil, come back to us from the movie in your head, you're in class!" Plus, she'd get angry if I didn't immediately understand what she wanted of me. Now she couldn't get angry because then she'd have to be angry at herself too. And how could she, when she didn't realize that she was wrapped up in her own movie? I said again, only louder this time:

"Miss..."

"Yes?"

"What's the matter?"

"What do you mean, what's the matter? I could ask you the same thing. What's the matter with you, Emil?"

"Nothing."

"Well then, like you, nothing's the matter."

I didn't want to say she was lying, because it's not nice to talk to the teacher that way, so I said:

"I hear…"

"What? That it's snowing? Like in your homework?!"

"No, no, that…your… heart...is…racing!"

Naturally, there was no way to avoid disaster. And the disaster was mine.

She turned beetroot red. And the redness spread to her ears and neck. But the roar of laughter in the classroom had only just begun! Even Professor Nikola laughed and said:

"I didn't know that Emil was capable of teasing, and at the teacher's expense too…"

I couldn't hear anything anymore from the uproar in the classroom. Professor Nikola bit his lower lip, as if trying to stop himself from laughing. It was only the teacher who didn't find it funny, and neither did I.

"Shame on you!" she began. "When we want to be rude, oh then we're loud! Then we find our tongue! But when it's answering a question in class or homework, then we don't know a thing. We do the wrong homework. We have cloth ears. It's me you want to provoke and make a fool of? Me you want to mock?! That's the thanks I get for all the effort I've put into you!"

I could feel my ears burning.

"You know, if you don't have anything clever to say, and clearly you haven't, you can leave the classroom. Anyway, we've got shorter classes today because of the meeting. You leave first to avoid the crush of children on the staircase. And don't forget to take your butterflies!"

For those who don't know, there's also a different kind of silence. There's loud silence. It comes after bad weather or a storm. You can see and feel its after-affects all around. Only this time it wasn't branches, leaves, rubbish or dead birds. This time it was her words that trailed behind me to the sound of my shoes: *clomp, clomp*...

The whole class was looking at them. They always looked as if they were seeing them for the first time. I didn't need eyes in the back of my head to know that.

"You've certainly got a way with you, Gordana", I heard Professor Nikola say. "I don't think he's even aware of what he said and there's nothing nasty or mocking about him, in fact, if we're honest, he didn't say anything bad. What he said about the heart was...nice. Don't be so hard on him, for heaven's sake!"

"Be quiet and don't interfere! This is my class!" she said through gritted teeth.

"Did you see his face when you lost your temper? It broke my heart,"

Professor Nikola said lowering his voice. I didn't wait for her answer. I didn't care. I said to myself *goodbye* and closed the door behind me.

The sky was huge, but my steps had never been smaller. It was as if the whole sky had turned into one big grey, heavy cloud. It almost scraped the tallest branches on the trees. I left the butterflies on the little playground wall. Maybe they'll see their friends tonight. That's what I hoped. When I creaked opened the playground's iron gate, it sighed sadly. Or maybe that's just how it seemed. Or maybe that was me. I walked down the street and heard somebody call out to me:

"Well, well! What a coincidence! Look who's here."

I turned around. Facing me was the person *It's Good to Do Good* called a dealer.

Piggybank

THE AUDI was racing down the road. Sitting inside were Instantly and me. That's what the man with the missing tooth was called. Instantly. I'd never heard of a name like that before, and told him so, I even asked what his last name was. I told him my last name was Vidić, and said: What's yours? He told me to shut up, he was the one asking the questions here, not me! So, I immediately shut my mouth, just when I thought we were getting along. This time he hadn't asked for a favour, he'd just told me to cross the street and keep my mouth shut. As if that was a problem for me. As if I was a chatterbox and he had to make a point of saying it. I was surprised and thought to myself: a first name like that must have a special last name to go with it! Nothing less. He'd told me to put my bag in the car and get in, saying that if I by any chance screamed like the day before yesterday downstairs, it would be the last scream of my life. Nobody had ever played Instantly for a sucker or shafted him! That person had yet to be born! Stupid idiot! And with those words we'd set off into the unknown.

We crossed several intersections and lots of roads. We didn't stop anywhere and we didn't talk. Maybe because his mobiles kept ringing - he had three of them. He was brief and rude when he answered the calls: "Aha, OK, same place like last time, it's all the fucking same, what are you, stupid?! Right, no sweat!" Once he shouted at somebody: "Fuck off! Not in three days, tonight! You know that I fucked somebody up because of you! *I want the rest tonight*! I put my trust in you, you fucking cunt!"

Then he switched off his mobiles and we drove in silence again.

I have a mobile too, but it's mostly silent. Because mum told me not to show it to anybody. That little novelty, as she called it, cost a pretty penny. Somebody might steal it. Uncle Jakov gave it to me because he had several of them, like Instantly. Mum says he's a businessman. The more business you have, the more mobiles you need. I remember the day I got it because I didn't manage to thank him. And for some reason it was important to do that. That day, the words wouldn't come out. I was scared when I took it. I looked at my uncle's black eyes and polished shoes but didn't say anything. I tried to guess what size shoe he wore and thought it would be nicer to have a new shoebox instead of the mobile he was giving me. Because I know everything there is to know about boxes, but nothing about mobiles. I nodded my head while he explained how to turn it on, turn it off, tap in the numbers but...I didn't say anything. Mum was terribly upset about that:

"Emil, how long are you going to keep that up?" she shouted. "Say thank you! What's the problem in saying THANK YOU? I mean, it's not as if Uncle Jakov is a stranger."

No, he wasn't a stranger. So, I said *thank you*, but to myself. Because I don't know what my problem is. How could I know when even my own mother doesn't seem to know? I think that most times people don't know what their problem is. They understand other people's problems better than their own. That's why you go to a doctor, for him to tell you what's wrong. I go with mum to the doctor, but I still don't know what my problem is. Maybe that's because it's not just one problem, it's several. On the other hand, I seldom catch cold. My heart is fine. It's just my feet that are a problem, and I'm tongue-tied. I don't know why that is. Maybe Miss Vjeka has a problem too, because she thinks she's good, but she isn't. And Professor Antun. Because he's blind but thinks he can do everything himself. I just know that sometimes I can talk and sometimes I can't. Sometimes the words come out, and sometimes they don't. I didn't know why I needed a mobile since I wasn't allowed to tell anybody that I had one. If only I could at least boast about it, since my grades were nothing to boast about. The more she said *say thank you* the more my head drooped. That's number 1. Plus, I was afraid I wouldn't know how to shake hands with him. And that I'd look stupid. Why all the fuss, I kept thinking, when Uncle Jakov wasn't making a problem out of it.

"It's OK, Marina. I understand him better than I do those who talk a lot. He said thank you to himself, I know he did. He'll say it aloud when he can. No problem."

He said it a few times, no problem. So, what's the problem, I asked myself.

Then Auntie Zrinka piped up. In my opinion she's got a problem too, but she likes pretending that she doesn't, and most of all she likes pointing at my problem. She'd kept quiet throughout that talk about the mobile and saying thank you. She never paid any attention to me anyway. If there was something she wanted to say to me, she'd do it through mum, as if I weren't there. I don't think that's called a problem with her vision, because I'm not that small and I'm not invisible. Her explanation was this: I supposedly never say anything, so who could follow my *mental track?!* I remembered the word but I'm sure she didn't say it properly. A track doesn't mean anything. I know because afterwards I asked mum to explain the word to me, but she said: "It doesn't mean anything, forget it, Auntie Zrinka talks nonsense when she's angry."

Maybe she was thinking of a metal trap. The kind they use to catch mice and rabbits. It's true that I like animals, but I don't know what that would have to do with me. And people traps don't exist. There are only word traps. Words sometimes get trapped in my mouth. That sometimes also happens to other children in class when the teacher asks them a question, but the trap disappears as soon as the questioning is over. Mine stays in my mouth even after that. Who knows why?

Raising her voice, Auntie Zrinka said that Uncle Jakov would never have raised a child properly with the kind of useless attitude we'd just seen. If the two of them had had children, it would have been a disaster. 'If the two of them had had children!' she said twice. Uncle Jakov looked at her - you could hear his heart sinking...like a stone tossed into the sea. He said that it was a good thing then that the two of them didn't have children because, he agreed with her, he would have certainly ruined them. He, unlike her, was born to ruin everything he touched. So it was lucky that they didn't have children! - he repeated, twice.

This was met with silence. Everybody had turned the sound off in their mouth. Then Auntie Zrinka abruptly stood up, looked at me and said in front of everybody that this situation with me was enough to drive anybody crazy. It had become intolerable!

"What?" mum asked. "What's Emil got to do with anything? What's the matter with you?"

"Ask him, not me. Because nothing is the matter with me! Tell him to stop gaping at me! Out of everybody in the room it's always me he picks to stare at!" she exploded. "Tell him to stop! Tell him it's rude to stare at people!" she told mum even though I was in the room and she could have told me, but she didn't, because she never talked to me. Then, sniffling and blowing her nose into her hanky, she ran to the toilet.

"What's the matter with her? Is it PMS?" mum asked with some surprise, turning to Uncle Jakov.

"She's got PMS every day, especially when things don't go her way. I don't know if she's told you, but we've been arguing about children for days. That's why she reacted like that. After all these years, I'm prepared to adopt. I've had my fill of doctors and clinics. She's not for it. She says she doesn't want somebody's else's child. She doesn't want bad genes. She doesn't want a problematic kid. As if having a child of your own is any guarantee that you'll be spared all that. Yesterday I told her that she'd prefer to have children exhibited on a shelf, in a shop, like a package of flour or bottle of oil. All sterile, with labels and desirable traits, from eye colour to famous genes, we wouldn't want to leave anything to chance or to the cheap mistakes of nature. I tell you, Marina, your sister is becoming a tiresome perfectionist. And I told her so..."

"You shouldn't have spoken to her like that, Jakov, you know how sensitive she is when it comes to children..."

"And what about me? Am I not entitled to be sensitive? Was I supposed to keep quiet and suffer her finger-pointing at my imagined guilt, present and future? Sometimes I think that she's just jealous of the good relationship I have with Emil, because she herself is incapable of even getting close to him. But there's always a way, you just have to make an effort. Just so you know, I've had enough of her slinging mud at the family. It's as if she's just waiting for all of us to get together, so that she can start hitting out where it hurts most. And as for genes, I sometimes wonder if the two of you were born of the same mother…"

That was how the story of the mobile I got as a present ended that day.

Mum taught me how to call and how to answer if she phoned me. It took days even though she claimed it was easy since I had only one person on my contact list. I could have added another person, if only for texting, but typing is a problem for me. The letters come out doubled. All I needed was for the recipient to say: "Look at how that imbecile texted me!"

Mum never calls me when I'm at school. The phone is just in case of any urgent, unpredictable need. That's what she said. I wasn't sure if this now was such a case. Because what was I going to say to her? That I was in the car with Instantly? That maybe we were coming home? But what if we weren't? I hadn't asked him where we were going. Because what if he mentioned some unknown place? What then? And I had clearly heard that stone rolling around inside him. It was louder than that time in the lobby. Who's Instantly? mum would certainly ask if I phoned. What could I tell her? That I hadn't a clue? All I knew was that he was afraid of the dentist, like me, and that he had three mobiles, like Uncle Jakov. And what conclusion could you draw from that? None. That's what I was thinking as we drove in an unknown direction.

"Do you know where the two of us are going now?" Instantly finally asked. I shook my head. "You don't, eh? Well, we're going straight to your building. And then upstairs. Who's at home right now?"

What a relief to hear that he was driving me home. It was only then, when he took off his sunglasses, that I saw one of his eyes was swollen, and there was something purple under the other. Instead of answering, I pointed at his disfigured face.

"Mind your own business and answer the question! If you don't play ball, I'll fix your face like they fixed mine! You hear me?! I asked you, who's in the house?" he said, grimacing in pain and touching his swollen eye.

"Nobody."

"Speak up!!!" he said, a bit of spittle flying into the air. "So, nobody?! Where are the old folks?"

I only had mum and she was young and pretty. Instantly said again, his eyes boring into the rear-view mirror:

"You've clammed up, huh? I'm asking you who lives there: your mother, father, gran…"

I shook my head.

"You mean to say that somebody like you, with a screw loose, lives on his own, goes to school on his own, cooks lunch on his own, and all that?"

"No."

"Then what?"

"Mum…works."

"Where does she work?"

"At…the…stall"

"She owns a stall?"

I shook my head.

"Then what is she?"

"A… seamstress."

"Aha…So she's a seamstress at a stall. OK, then listen carefully. I'm going to go to your old lady and have her make me the most expensive suit there is. She's going to make me hundreds of expensive suits if you don't give me back what's mine! She's going to spend her whole life sewing for me, you get it? You cocky little shithead! You're fucked if you don't give it back …"

"She…sells…greeting…cards…decorations…little…fir…trees…little…cribs…", by some miracle the words started coming out of my mouth and I began listing all these things to make sure it was clear what kind of stall it was. But I didn't know how to explain that he'd have to come to our place if he wanted mum to measure him for a suit. I gazed thoughtfully through the car window, watched the traffic lights change colours and the road race away before my eyes.

"Cribs?" he said surprised, raising an eyebrow. "In this day and age, that kind of business is a loser! Some ten years ago, what your old lady is selling would've been a serious offence, but it would have brought in some money because anything that wasn't supposed to be sold on the market had added value. Yes! Why are you looking at me like that? You think Instantly is lying?! Such were the times, good for some, bad for others. Even then it was easier to deal than to believe in God! You just had to say – down with God! But the same guys who were walking all over God then, are kneeling at the altar now. I don't know what your old lady thinks about it, but I see that you haven't a clue. You're too young for these things..."

I don't know how we got onto the subject of religion, but I didn't want to tell him that *Catechism* says something different. Mum would agree with him about God, but our religion teacher wouldn't. OK, I don't really attend the religious studies class, not for real. Just sort of. Mum decided that I didn't need it. One nuisance less, she said. I sit there because they don't know what to do with me. I sit with the class, keep quiet and listen.

"You don't have to listen to anything or remember anything. Don't worry. Just be quiet," mum said.

I'm always quiet, but I can't not listen, especially if it's interesting. I'm very good at the stories we hear in religious studies. Better than in nature and social studies class. I know everything about the life of little Jesus who was born in a crib in the middle of winter. Unfortunately, it doesn't snow where he lived, but the animals warmed him at night with their breath. His real dad is God. The one who isn't real is called Joseph. I don't understand how somebody can have two dads when I don't have even one! I don't know who can explain that to me since mum won't. It always makes her angry. Both religious studies and dad. So, I'm just thinking.

"Look, nobody's gotten rich yet from that kind of business. If they had, I'd be selling those things myself. It would be much easier than...what I'm doing. But, let's get back to what we were talking about, OK? So, your old lady isn't at home. The flat is empty. Right?"

I nodded.

"You haven't mentioned your old man, I mean dad. I guess he doesn't exist, am I right?"

I nodded. I don't know how he guessed it right off.

"Great. So, it's just the two of us. You give me what's mine and we're done. OK?"

I shook my head because of course it wasn't OK.

"Don't try to be clever again, like that day with the rubbish! You think I'm stupid? You think I'm going to take your shit because you've got braces on your legs? Or because your old lady sells cribs? I don't give a fuck!"

"?!"

"What is it? Tell me! Talk or I'll yank the tongue out of your mouth!"

"I don't...have...the...key," I barely managed to say after unsticking my tongue from my palette. I quickly clamped shut my mouth so that he wouldn't see me pull my tongue back in, just in case.

"You don't? A big boy like you doesn't have the key? Assuming you're as old as you say you are. I wouldn't give you even half that age. You're all stunted, kid. Do you eat at all or do you just lie?"

"I...never...lie."

"No kidding! And I'm Mother Theresa, nice to meet you! C'mon, stop this crap! If I catch you screwing with me, you'll be in deep trouble!"

"I lost...a few."

"Lost a few what?"

"Keys."

"No problem. We'll get in without a key. You'll give me what isn't yours and that'll be the end of it."

I wondered how we would get in. Through the window? The balcony was closed and very high up. We weren't going to smash the glass pane, were we? I hadn't even broken the one in the lobby, although Mr. Franjo says otherwise, so I'm not about to smash ours! I can't climb in these shoes. But I can't do without them. No way! Which doesn't mean that I don't wish, more than anything, that I could...

My mouth was dry like in the summer when I don't drink enough water, and my trousers were sticking to my seat. I didn't move so that he wouldn't think I'd peed in my pants in fear. I was barely breathing, but all the same...I liked cars and going for drives, and it was interesting to hear what he was saying about God and cribs. Even if it was incorrect. Because maybe he never went to religious studies in school and so didn't know. I go and so I know. I know even if I don't have to know. On the other hand, nothing really ever happens to me. And when I say nothing, I mean – n o t h i n g. It's to the kiosk or the rubbish bin, and that's it, it's always the same. It's the same in the park too. Sometimes I sit on the bench and watch the children run around or fight...I imagine being among them. What it would look like: me with the other children, me with friends, me at a birthday party, me in a fight. I imagine somebody grabbing me and then me grabbing somebody, but that where my imagination stops.

Second, we don't have a car, even though mum has a licence. She sold it a long time ago because, she says, you can't eat a car when you're hungry. But you don't get anything out of sewing and working at the stall either. Except pneumonia. She had it twice. So, again, she would agree with Instantly on the subject of earnings and cribs. I imagined how wonderful it would be to go for a drive in the Audi every day. It smelled of leather. Of cigarettes. And of something sweet, like sweets. When we reached my street,

Instantly parked a bit further down, in the shade of the oak trees.

"You go in ahead of me. We'll act like we don't know each other. And don't try to be clever. I'll be watching your every move."

Aha, we'll play dumb, as *It's Good to Do Good* would say.

"I don't want anybody to see us together. You hear me?"

I nodded.

"Call the lift and wait. We'll go up together. We won't talk and don't you say one word to me until we reach your front door."

So, no window? What then? Luckily, *It's Good to Do Good* wasn't in her usual place on the balcony this time. She always used it as a kind of observation post. She knew everybody's comings and goings! Just in case, I pulled the hood over my head to shield myself against the wind and make myself as invisible as I could. Even though that's impossible when you're wearing such stupid shoes...

The lobby was empty and the lift was on the ground floor. We went up together, pretending not to know each other. I looked down at the floor and he looked at the mirror that hung on the side. Whistling some song, he pulled tight his leather jacket and sucked air in through the gap where he used to have a tooth. I was still worried about how he planned to open the door without a key. As soon as we neared the entrance, Instantly checked the corridor up and down, cocked an ear, calmed the restless stone inside him and only then pulled two pieces of wire out of his jacket pocket. One was bigger than the other. He stuck first the one and then the other into the lock. A little to the left, a little to the right, and the door miraculously unlocked!

I just breathed in loudly. Then breathed out…

"See?" he replied, winking at me meaningfully.

You wouldn't believe what an ordinary piece of wire can do! I headed straight for my room. The piggybank was on the desk. I gave it to him and that should have been it. Full stop! The end!

"What are you playing at? As if I came here to play with your toys. Where is it!?"

I tapped the pink piggy with my finger.

"In the piggybank? Wow!" Now it was his turn to be surprised. "And where's the key to this piggy?"

I shook my head because…

Just then we heard mum come home and call out to me.

We looked at one another. Instantly put his index finger to his lips (*shhh*), then ran it across his throat (*grrrl*). I got it – if you talk, you're done for! Like in a crime movie. Except we weren't criminals. I was in my own flat, and Instantly had come to get what was his. I walked out of the room and left him behind the door.

"What are you doing here, Emil? Why was the door open?"

"I forgot to close it," I said because that was the honest truth. I hadn't thought about the door when I walked in with Instantly. I had the piggybank on my mind.

"That's not what I'm asking you, I'm…," she didn't finish, she immediately moved to other questions. "I didn't forget to lock the door this morning, did I? I'm becoming forgetful. Did you check if anything in the flat is missing? You didn't? What are you waiting for? Go and see if anything is missing! Why are you standing there like a sculpture! Move!"

"Everything seems to be OK. I don't know what's worth taking in this flat anyway. Who would want to break in here? By the way, how come you're home early? Why didn't you call me on the mobile and tell me that your class was cut short? Why did I give you the phone in the first place? To carry it around for decoration?" The questions kept coming hard and fast. "How was school? How did your butterflies do?" she asked, putting the bags of food on the table and the food in the refrigerator, but I didn't know which of her questions to answer.

"The teacher gifted me a 2," I said, sitting down at the table.

"What do you mean gifted?"

"She said that the subject had been winter not spring. As if I didn't know. I'm not stupid."

"Of course you're not. See, I knew exactly how it would go with those butterflies! And she imagines she is working with you by using an adapted programme? Where and how is she adapting to you? Or are you maybe supposed to adapt to her, to make it easier for her? I'll ask her that tomorrow!"

"..."

"What do I care if she does or doesn't have time to do her work? Does anybody ask me if I have time? I'm fed up with her constant moaning: she doesn't have time, she doesn't understand you, she's got some thirty other students to think about, your head is always in the clouds...I'd like to see her work at a stall. Eight hours out in the wind, and then eight hours threading a needle with hands like these."

"..."

"I couldn't care less about the grades, but...it's as if her tongue would fall off if she didn't make some kind of nasty remark. Not to mention that she's deaf to your needs. Not all children have the same needs, they're not like pie moulds."

"You're making apple pie?" I asked.

"No! I'm talking about mass production! The kind of children our schools produce today. And she's just a mass-produced teacher. Never mind, come to your mummy. Enough talk about her. You are my sweetest little biscuit in the whole world..."

She opened wide her arms and we held each other tight. She smelled of...apple strudel. My favourite dessert. And she felt warm and soft, like a freshly baked cake.

"Mmmmm...my specially produced little biscuit. I'm not giving you to anyone, not even for a perfect, faultlessly made biscuit."

"?!"

She ran her fingers through my hair the way I love, brushed it away from my forehead and gave me a loud kiss.

I love it when mum sits me on her lap, even though I'm already ten. Naturally I'm too big for such things, but who cares when we're alone. And nobody can see us. Not even Auntie Zrinka, who'd usually say that we were overdoing it because I'm not two years old or a baby anymore. Because if she had a child of her own, she'd never allow it. Spoiling a child like that. Parents have to raise their children with a firm hand. Mum just says she shouldn't talk about things she knows nothing about and has never experienced. When and if she ever has a child of her own, it'll be a different story. Children always remain children to their parents, even when they grow up and have children of their own.

Then she sighed, smiled and said:

"Are you hungry? Take those shoes off, put your slippers on and wash your hands, we're going to have lunch."

I wasn't hungry. I'm never hungry and that's that. Then I remembered Instantly. How was I going to explain to mum what he was doing in my room holding my piggybank? What was I going to tell her? That I'd promised something but later, as usual, forgot about it, and it complicated matters. Something like that, maybe?

I opened the door of my room, but he was nowhere to be seen. Not behind the door, not under the bed. And the piggybank was gone too. I didn't report it to mum. Naturally.

Supernova

I WAS sitting on my favourite bench in the park. I'd bought a lollipop at the kiosk and a pack of Smurf picture cards. Mum had given me twenty kunas. The lollipop cost two kunas, the pictures five. So, 5 + 2 = 7. And 20 – 7 = …?

The bad thing is that I can't count it because I don't have twenty fingers. The good thing is that the woman at the kiosk knows me by name and she's never once cheated me. She knows where I live, she knows mum's name and she knows why I'm in a class with children younger than me. On the other hand, I don't know a thing about her. Not her name, not her street. Not if she has a problem too. Nothing. But that doesn't stop her from asking me every time: how's school, how are your grades, how's your mum, where does your mum work, where's your father gone, does mum take you to see the doctor? Her favourite is: what do the doctors have to say about your problem?

Most of the time I don't say anything, I just wait for her to give me my change. Because I want to see if I got it right. It always ends with her looking away and turning her attention to the till or the other customers. Mum certainly wouldn't like it if she knew that the woman keeps asking me these questions. Because she doesn't like people sticking their noses into our affairs. Everybody, she says, has an itch somewhere that they can keep scratching until the end of their days. So let them scratch away and just leave us alone. But since she doesn't know anything about the kiosk woman and her questions, mum always says cheerfully:

"Incredible! Just as you lose faith in people, you suddenly see that values like honesty and kindness haven't died. Bravo!"

I don't tell her anything about the inquisitive kiosk woman, because it would make mum very angry and she would stop me from practising my social skills at the kiosk. She might go up to the woman and tell her what she thinks of her. Because mum doesn't let things ride. She says what she's got to say. Straight to your face. Let the chips fall where they may, she says. But I know that then that would be the end. Full stop. The other kiosk is much farther away and she'd never let me go there. I like this kiosk, the babble of voices, the patter of feet, the jingling of coins, the rustling of newspapers and the laughter of the kiosk lady when she sees her favourite customers. Like me.

But to get back to the bench.

I like it because it's got carvings on it. In the middle, on the part where I lean back, there's a big heart pierced with an arrow. I wanted to make something like that myself. To carve a heart, with my name and mum's name inside it. Naturally, with the hands I've got, it didn't go well. I tried for several days. I might even have succeeded if Mr. Franjo from our building hadn't stopped me. He appeared out of the blue and told me that I should be ashamed of myself, destroying public property like that. I thought: he needs new glasses. Was he blind or what? Couldn't he see that it was just an ordinary wooden bench? I told him that I wasn't destroying anything. I was just drawing. I was carving. I was exercising my fingers. I was good at it. At drawing.

He said not to play dumb! Unless I wanted him to mention the lobby windows again. Did I want him to mention them again? I shook my head. No way! It's beyond me how he can keep mentioning something I didn't do. He talked about those windows so often that I was about to believe that I had done something that I hadn't. It's true that I had a ball in my hands that day. But I didn't do anything with it, I just held it. Until those two came along and grabbed it from me. They laughed a little, I'm not sure if it was at me or at the ball, and then they kicked it. One of them said: "We'll show you how it's done, because you're a clumsy retard and can't do it yourself. Here, look, like this!" The ball soared high up in the air and flew straight into the front window of our building. Then they ran away. I was left holding the ball, all alone, looking at the broken pieces of glass, while Mr. Franjo, who had just appeared, started lecturing me about how badly brought up I was.

And now he went on talking about it even though I had indicated with my head that I didn't want to hear another word on the subject.

I may have forgotten about it, but he hadn't, he said. He might be old, but his brain was sharper than many a young person's. If he caught me engaged in such scandalous behaviour again, he'd take me to the police, and from there – as we all know – it's prison! He didn't care who I was, what I was, or what my diagnosis was. Yes,…yes…most people, unfortunately, are born with diagnoses. Most people, if you consider that we live in rotten times. Totally perverse times. It wasn't like that in his day. Young men went into the army and came out as adults. Just look at these rotten young people who don't know what to do with themselves. All of them inept. They traipse around with a bottle of alcohol in their hand. They destroy benches. It's all so pitiful and sad. It's the twilight of civilization. These diagnoses mean that some people have very messed up heads, others, less so. He said I belonged to the first group and was different from others in that I was incapable of controlling my aggressive outbursts. Never mind, we were all equal before the law! Was he clear enough or did he have to spell it out for me again? No problem, he'd repeat it if I needed time to understand what he was saying.

I started to cry. Unlike mum, who never cries, I often cry. She cries too, but in a different way.

I didn't want him to repeat all those words I didn't understand, I wanted him to leave me alone. The only word I understood was prison. I clutched the small knife in my pocket that I'd taken from home and cried. I looked down at my feet and cried. He went on and on, lecturing me about the damage I'd done and again said that it's only aggressive people who go for the knife and get up to such things. That's how it starts, with windows and benches, and it ends with...I didn't hear what it ends with because just then a man walked in. As soon as he opened his mouth, I recognized Mikula's voice.

Mikula lives on the ground floor of our building. Mama always greets him nicely, especially since he wrote a newspaper article about the working conditions of people who sell things at stalls. Mum said this about him: "it's terrible to be a grown man, like Mikula, have a university degree in your pocket and be unemployed, live in your mum's flat and live off your mum's pension." That's what *my* mum said about him and *his* mum. Maybe Mikula thought differently about living with his mum. Because I don't always agree with what *my* mum thinks either.

"Mr. Franjo, why not leave the boy alone?" Mikula said, walking over to us. He had on a tracksuit and the trainers he wears for his daily ten-kilometre run, to keep fit, he says. "What's…fit?" I asked the day he bought them and left the empty shoebox on the wall by the rubbish. We'd run into each other by the wheelie bin, where else, when I was throwing out the two disgusting bags of rubbish.

"It means to keep in shape, to be healthy!" he said, taking a deep breath and pumping up his muscles as if to show them off. Reaching for his empty shoe box because I didn't have one like it in my collection, I asked if that meant that I wasn't healthy. I run only in my dreams. Did that count?

He looked at me but said nothing, though he's not usually quiet. He was tongue-tied and just looked at me. That happens to me too sometimes, out of the blue. The words won't come out. The only sound came from the talk of the beer can that the wind had pushed into a pile of fallen leaves.

"No…no…that's not what I meant, Emil. You completely misunderstood me," he said, finally letting out the air he had been holding in, like a punctured balloon. "It has nothing to do with you. There are lots of people who don't run, but they're still healthy. I just like to run."

"Me too," I said.

Then we fell silent again. The sound inside his chest was like that empty beer can carried away by the wind.

"So, I'm healthy?" I asked, because I was talking pretty well, which doesn't happen often.

"Emil, I'm not a doctor, I'm a journalist, but it's not a problem, we can talk about anything you like, only some other time, not now. Right now, I'm in a hurry. I have to finish my run. Bye, kid. See you around."

I nodded, and he added that I was free to take that shoebox and as soon as he bought another pair of shoes he'd bring me the box himself so that I wouldn't have to take it out of the rubbish. He smiled and ran off.

And now here he was! Standing next to us, panting and barely getting the words out. "Don't you have…something better…to do…than to harass kids in the park? What kind of…vocabulary is that …to explain the notion of good and bad to the boy? Have you become a psychiatrist in your… retirement?! If…the theory about…diagnoses is correct, I'd like to know…what's yours?"

"You'd like to know! You don't say?! Who's asking you?! Why are you butting in, you good-for-nothing! Get out of here! Run! Beat it! Go twiddle your thumbs. You're obviously good at that!"

"It's not my fault if I the only thing I'm good at in life is twiddling my thumbs. It's because of you and your sort that I'm like this! You pushed me into it!"

"Is that so? How, pray tell?!"

"All these years you did just fine. While you could. Moving from one company to another. Skimming them off all nice and legal and filling your pockets. You milked one after the other dry, like a dairy cow. Until everything went to fucking hell! It's because of people like you that everything in this country has gone to pot. Whatever was good under communism is gone! And whatever was bad has turned into a living horror! Into roving zombies! And now somebody like you finds it fit, from your cushy life, to lecture me and this boy? You, of all people! Have you no shame? This boy will never steal or destroy as much public property as you have. And I won't either! You've laid waste to everything for generations to come! You bunch of thieves!"

I stopped crying, straining my frightened ears. I didn't know who scared me more, Mikula or Mr. Franjo. Now they were right up close to each other, except Mikula was younger, stronger and taller, and I had no doubt who would win if there was a punch-up. Except I don't like boxing. Not in life and not on TV. At home I take the remote and change the channel, but how could I turn off the sound and picture here?

They shoved each other, their heads drawing closer and closer. I broke out in a sweat as if I was the one at risk. Fortunately, some passers-by stepped in. They somehow managed to separate the two of them and pull them back like the dogs I sometimes see foaming at the mouth and being held back on a short leash by their owners. Mikula kept yelling: "You rotten old bastard! You political bootlicker! You've stolen everything! You and your kind in power!" And Mr. Franjo shot back: "You piece of journalistic shit! You earn your money lolling around! I'll take you to court for slander!" "That's OK by me," Mikula shouted, "no problem at all, but first I'll send over some investigators to look into the source of your assets!"

And that's how I gave up carving. Though I still think there's nothing bad about saying that you love somebody on a bench. Left on the bench since then are my two unfinished scribbles, M + E…That's all.

Mum always lets me stay in the park for a bit. Nobody was there today. The pathway was deserted and the sky was grey. I thought about snow and how everybody says it's impossible it will be like last year. I so wanted to hear the snowflakes gather high up in the sky again, like the rustling wings of butterflies.

"Of all the seasons, it's winter that has the strongest arms and legs," I said to the teacher, trying to explain why winter was my favourite season and why in my clay model it looked like a white giant.

"What's this?" she asked when she saw it. "What do you mean arms and legs?"

Since I couldn't explain it properly aloud, I said it to myself, that I love looking at the park in the winter. And what do I see? I see winter hug nature with its invisible arms and legs. And what does nature do then? It falls asleep and dreams. Waiting to wake up. Like me. I dream that I'm as strong as winter. But when I wake up, I realize that I'm like nature waiting to wake up from the white giant's embrace. I said all this to myself, so nobody heard it. She said that the assignment hadn't been to create a character from a fairy tale or a yeti from the Himalayas, but to portray winter. Why did I always complicate everything?

I hunched my shoulders and pulled my cap down over my head. It was getting colder, but I didn't budge from the bench. I looked at the tree dreaming and listened to the ice cracking in the puddles. That's when I caught sight of Professor Antun, the blind man from the first floor whose rubbish I took out on Saturdays.

"Is that you there, Emil? Oh yes, I know that it is..." he said when he reached the bench, tapping it with his white stick.

That was something that always surprised me about him. Because I hadn't said a word. I was barely breathing. And still, he knew I was there. In addition to his hearing, he had a great nose for people.

I nodded my head and said: "Aha.."

"What wonderful air! It's particularly crisp today. It hurts my lungs to breathe, but I simply had to come out and stretch my legs. I haven't been out of the house for days. And that's not good for your bones and muscles. It's important to move, Emil, for as long as you can, especially for the two of us. What? I told you to move, not run. To walk. You understand? What do you mean, why? Because of our handicap. Otherwise, we let it rule our body. Lord, what questions you've got this morning! Of course you're healthy. Nobody says you're sick if you can't run. There are different ways we can move and we don't need legs for that."

"???"

"Now, tell me, have you heard the latest song I've been playing these last few days? You see, music doesn't have legs but it finds its way to people's ears all the same. Admittedly, not everybody is attuned to it, that's something we have to live with…"

I had heard the song, and I told him so. The professor had once explained to me that it didn't matter if you couldn't see, that there were letters and notes for the blind. You just had to touch them on a special kind of paper. Once you learned them, it was easy. Some people, even though their senses are in perfect working order, are disabled when it comes to colours, sounds, signs. Their instrument for receiving stimuli from the environment, he explained again, doesn't work properly.

And then he suddenly said this:

"Well now, since you're in the mood to talk, let's take that a bit further. Alright? I know you're still young and maybe don't think about these things, but have you ever wondered why we come into this world? Why we are here?"

Hmmm…Mostly I think about wanting a brother or sister and I always wonder why they haven't come. I stopped for a second, I didn't want him to say that I wasn't trying and that I gave up too quickly, but he rushed on, as if he didn't even expect me to answer.

"You're silent, so let me tell you this as well: most people walk through the world unaware of what lies behind the visible and tangible. I know that, given your incredible hearing, you realize this yourself. You see, these things are like sheet music. In order to know what they say, you have to decipher them. Use the right key. In music we use the treble clef and the bass clef. You don't read the notes in one key the same way you do in another. The rules are different. And it's the same with the world. It lies here before us like a sheet of paper with a hidden melody on it, but not everybody is capable of deciphering or hearing it."

"???"

"That's why most people rumble through the world like a crowd of deafmen aware only of their own noise."

"!!!"

"Or the wind! Do you feel it? With me, it's not just the cold that I feel. Everything is like a deluge of auditory shudders, if you get my meaning. You see, even from that there is something to be learned about…movement. The rowdy crowd chooses instead to behave like blades of grass. It learns how to bend. How to drop roots and stubbornly resist. Thus missing out on the possibility of soaring and learning new things. Remaining aware of only the physical aspect of existence."

It was a good thing I was sitting! Otherwise, I would have collapsed...*fa-thud*!

It felt as if I was seeing Professor Antun for the first time. He had never talked to me like that before, maybe he did with mum. Because...

...mum says that the professor is becoming increasingly tiresome and prone to the philosophising of an old man. You can no longer ring his doorbell and ask him if he needs anything without him starting to talk at great length and in great detail. About all and sundry. About what's important and what isn't. Just when she's in a hurry or late for work, he starts talking. He's like that because he's lonely and helpless, but he won't hear of going to an old people's home. Stubbornness is his main trait. He says old people's homes are homes for the dying! As if there's a place where you don't have to die. That's why the elderly fall victim to crooks. Like that lady from the floor above. A couple of those people who offer God from door to door rang her bell (?!). They made their offer sound as if God was part of a package of additional health insurance. (?!) They sensed her need for company. Her fear of loneliness. They falsely offered her charity until she loosened her purse strings and signed her name to whatever they wanted. But she wound up in an old people's home all the same. They are still offering all sorts of things, but now they've made her flat their base. And that's not right, mum says. Whoever is watching us from above isn't stupid!

"You mean God is watching us after all? That's what the religion teacher says too," I said, surprised by her words, knowing that this was not something she liked discussing with me.

"Your religion teacher can claim what she wants. Unlike her, I make no claims. Except that I did not use the word God. I'd be more likely to use the term *the intelligence of the universe*. But you're too young for me to discuss that with you. It's arrogant to suggest that there's only one truth, but that's what all religions in the world do. You see, this grey mass in our head is called the brain. Who is to say that the universe isn't just a brain? But a big one. An incredibly big and powerful one. So big that you can't embrace it with your senses or reason. Just as an ant can't fathom the ground it's walking on. It's such a vast topic that you can't understand it, biscuit, so let's stop here. Look: all those stars, planets, black holes...maybe they are the brain's impulses, its signs of activity. And people are like particles of dust... turning the little wheels of the universe's organism."

That's called being left speechless! For a long time afterwards, I kept repeating her words and wrote them down so I wouldn't forget them, especially the *intelligence of the universe* bit. But everything she said was unimaginable. As unimaginable as it might be to an ant. So, I asked myself:

If the universe is a brain, then whose head is it in? And where is that head? Whose shoulders does it rest on?

But to get back to the professor:

"Excuse me. I don't know what got over me," he coughed, snapping me out of my musing. "I overdid it a bit. I know I did. And more than just a bit. Maybe, as your mother says, I'm lonely after all and I pounce on the first victim I find to talk to. I almost forgot how old you are, that you're a child. Please, forget whatever I said and don't say anything to your mother. She'd be angry if she knew that I was boring you with things that are not for a boy your age. I'm sorry if I upset or confused you."

"Do you want to play …the listening game?" I asked, because I didn't know what else to say or what to think.

"Alright. The two of us are living proof that eyesight only impedes listening. Then again, you are a special case. You're special in yourself. OK, I'll start first and you follow. The bird on the branch to the right, it's pecking at something on the bark."

I heard it. Now it was my turn:

"Behind the bend in the road…there's a dog coming. It's panting. It's straining …at the leash.

"Well done! And did you hear how the twig on the tree to our left just snapped?"

I did.

"There's…a cat coming!" I blew the words into my gloves.

"A cat? Where? I don't hear anything. If only that incredible ability of yours could be put to good use somewhere, but I don't know where. It's supernatural!"

There was nothing supernatural about it and I didn't know if the professor knew about the problems I had in school. An adapted programme. Mathematics couldn't be worse. Writing so-so. Nature and social studies, a disaster. Religious studies, not bad but it doesn't count. PE, zero (for now). Reading, OK, but could be better. Nobody in school asks me what I hear. Unless I tell them myself. But it never turns out well, it always ends with: "Look at the imbecile, he lies and laughs for no reason."

When the cat finally reached us, it rubbed itself against my leg. They say on TV that cats have certain special senses of their own. They can sense when something's about to happen. Who knows what they see when they sniff around my feet, but Miss Vjeka's cats do the same thing. It was only then that the professor heard it. I didn't tell him that I could hear more and further away than that. Mum says there are some things I should keep to myself. It's not good to crow for no reason. Or to cast pearls before swine. She explained the thing about the pearls like this: my hearing is a pearl but some people are swine that wallow in the mud and trample on pearls. Because a pig doesn't know what a pearl is.

I rose from the bench and told the professor that I had to go home now. Mum would be looking for me. "Be careful on the road," he said. I waved, though I knew he couldn't see it. I imagined that he felt me wave goodbye and made my way out of the park.

At first, I only thought I saw the familiar black Audi on the side of the road. But as I got nearer, I had no doubt whose car it was and who was sitting inside it, his elbow jutting out of the window.

"You wanna go for a drive, Emil? I'll get you home in five minutes," he said, his tone easy-going, as if talking to an old friend. He'd covered his eyes with dark sunglasses.

I nodded. Because that was the only chance I'd get to go for a drive. Because I'd decided not to be a coward. Fear is our greatest enemy, if you're afraid you don't get anywhere, it says in *Catechism*. Which isn't quite true, because Jesus wasn't afraid of anything, and we know how he ended up. I heard the stone in Instantly roll. I heard it but ignored it. His stone, his problem. I had nothing to do with it. We'd resolved the matter of the little packets. So, there was no problem. *Relax, Emil*, I said to myself.

We set off. He adjusted the rear-view mirror so he could see me better on the back seat. He turned on the radio. I knew he was going to say something important when he cleared his throat and coughed. That's how all important conversations seem to start. With clearing the throat.

"I had to smash open your piggybank to get out…those things. You understand? It was a great hiding place, but how did you think I'd get them out without the key? You didn't use your brain, did you?"

I shook my head. In honesty, the only thing I'd been thinking about was finding a good hiding place for the packets.

"And you know what happened afterwards? When I smashed open the piggybank I didn't find the same number of packets that I'd given you. Why do you think that was?"

"?!"

"Listen, I'm not saying you stole anything. You don't look like a thief or a crook, but maybe some fell out, along the way…"

I quickly shook my head, several times.

"I'm telling you, some are missing. And what's missing costs a lot of money!" he pressed on.

"I don't…have…money. It's…not…my fault."

"Let me cut to the quick. There's a way for you to pay me back for the damage," he went on, as if he wasn't hearing me say that with the packets gone, I had nothing. He sucked the air in through the gap left by his missing tooth and said: "Look, you'll do a few, let's call them favours for me, like the first time, and pay off your debt that way. OK?"

No, it wasn't OK! But I didn't say anything. I just kept quiet. I kept quiet, thinking that I was no good at negotiating, at business and promises. Because I forget things. Especially homework. Thank goodness Natalia didn't have such a problem with her memory.

"You're not saying anything, which means you agree," he said, pressing the horn to signal to the car in front that the traffic light had turned green. "And if you refuse, you'll have to pay for the loss in the form of money. Understand?"

"I...don't...have...money," I could barely hear myself say.

"I know. We've already deduced that. And to tell you the truth, I don't really feel like letting you settle your debt by having your old lady sew me suits for the rest of her life. Who knows, maybe she's not that great a seamstress, maybe I wouldn't be happy with her work. And then what? I like nice clothes. Expensive, good clothes. Clear?"

I nodded.

"So this is what we'll do, you will be given fresh packets which you will deliver to a certain place. I will take you there. Obviously, with feet like that, you're not going to walk across town. So, you'll take the packets, leave them, or deliver them, depending on what I tell you to do. It's simple. But nobody can know about it, or even that we know each other. If you tell anybody about me, first, I'll say you're lying and that you've got a screw loose, and second, you're fucked. Clear?"

"I never...lie."

"I know. I've already heard you make that earth-shattering statement. And have you heard me say that I'm Mother Theresa? You have! So, stop saying *never* and stop playing dumb. Because I can play dumb too. There's a first time for everything. In case you didn't know, sometimes it's a good thing to lie..."

"Tonko...lies too."

"Who's Tonko?

"From...my class."

"I don't know what you're talking about and I have no time for your stories from school. Some other time. We've got work to do. I thought you could start now. You'll pay off your debt sooner."

I thought about the debt. Who was responsible for it, to whom and why? My responsibility was to study. The teacher's was to work with me according to the adapted programme. Mum's was to take care of me. Instantly's was to distribute the packets. What did that have to do with me and what should I do now?

"And what...should...I do...now?"

Instantly parked the car in a huge parking lot. In front of us was Supernova, the big department store. I had planned to buy my trainers there if Mum let me do PE Instantly told me to go inside and just act normal. (As if I didn't anyway!) He gave me a packet and said that I should sit down on the bench in front of the Adidas shop.

"Can you read? A-di-das!"

Of course I could read! And anyway, even if I couldn't, it was the only brand with three slanted parallel stripes. Like the tail of a crocodile!

"Alright. Sitting on the bench in front of that shop is my...client. Go over to him."

He described his client: woollen hat, beard, glasses, thin, trembling hands, ugly as sin.

"There's nothing to be afraid of, just act cool and relaxed. Slowly, calmly, take out the packet, pretend you're looking at the store window or waiting for somebody and give it to him. No talking, no touching, nothing. Just hand it over. Understand? Then come back to the car and I'll drive you home."

I did as I was told. I'd never been to the department store before because we didn't have a car, and Supernova was far away. At the end of town. I spotted the client from far away. He was fidgety and kept scratching himself. I sat down next to him. I looked around as Instantly had told me to do. Ringing out in the department store was the Christmas song: *Jingle bells, jingle bells...*

That was when I noticed that the client kept stealing a glance at me, was sniffling and wiping his nose with his jacket sleeve as if he had a cold. Maybe the packet was medicine for some illness. A medicine you couldn't get on prescription at the pharmacy.

And then...just as I'd slipped my hand into my pocket to take out the packet and give it to him, *It's Good to Do Good* walked out of the store.

"Emil?!", she said in surprise, opening wide her eyes, planting her feet firmly in front of us. "Well...Good Morning to you. Who'd ever expect to see you here?"

Her *Good Morning* really got on my nerves. How can every morning be a good one? Anyway, she didn't care about my morning being good, she just likes to stick her nose where it doesn't belong, says Mum.

"Are you here with your mum?"

I didn't say anything.

"You didn't come this far without her, did you?"

Now she turned her gaze onto the client, giving him the once-over. The client, naturally, played dumb, as if the two of us didn't know each other, which wasn't far from the truth. We didn't know each other. I didn't know who he was, where he lived or what he was called. I didn't think he knew anything about me, either.

I nodded my head. That turned out to work in my favour, though actually I was nodding in answer to her second question, that I had come without mum.

"Oh, I see...," I knew she thought my answer was to her first question. "Indeed, it would have been impossible for you to come all the way here on your own. Even by bus. OK, don't move from here, so you don't get lost. I don't know why your mum takes you to places like this, they're not for children like you. She's sure to be with someone in a café or boutique! Right? You just don't want to admit it. I know, you're sitting here like a poor little orphan, defending your mum. I hope you didn't try to drag yourself up the escalator? That would be very dangerous. Imagine if you tripped and fell. Whose fault would that be? I mean, your mum is a pretty irresponsible person and if you ask me..."

Just then the client went crazy! Because of her non-stop talking, even though nobody had asked her anything. Even though I hadn't opened my mouth to talk to her. Even though I just stared at my shoes and kept quiet.

"Hey, fuck off, old lady! You're a pain! Whaddya want? Can't you see that the kid is waiting for his mother? She's in the store. I saw her. And here you are crapping to him about her! You're getting on my nerves, and on his too, for sure!"

He was right. She was getting...on my...whatever.

It's Good to do Good was shocked. She stood there, staring first at me, then at him, then at me, then at him again. She tried hard to connect the dots. What was going on here? I barely knew myself. I wasn't sure if, in the end, she was any the wiser, but she quickly turned on her heels and strode off. There was no time to waste. I took what I had out of my pocket and handed it to the client. He took it without a word, blew his nose like a whale, stood up and vanished.

I just sat there for a while, thinking of *It's Good to Do Good*. Maybe she was waiting for me somewhere so that she could follow me. Maybe she was lurking somewhere, like in a movie. I had no choice but to get up and slowly head for the exit.

Instantly was waiting for me in the same place.

"Where the fuck have you been? I was already beginning to think that some shit had happened!"

Not counting my meeting with *It's Good to Do Good*, everything else had been more or less straightforward. So much so that I wondered what was really behind it all. He could have easily done without me. Plus, nobody would have asked him if he had come with his mum. Or if he had dragged himself onto the escalator.

I sank into the back seat of the Audi, eager for us to leave. In the end, the drive lulled me to sleep. When we arrived, he woke me up saying:

"Get off your ass, kid! We're here."

He dropped me off two blocks away, in the shade of the old oak trees.

Professor Antun

I CRIED a little the day I got sick and had to say home. That's what you say when you've got the flu or a cold and sniffle. But when you have weak hands and feet like me, then you don't say you're sick. You say you've got a problem. And a problem and sickness are two different things. Because of my problem I go to see several doctors, like Auntie Lilia and Uncle Mario and some others whose names I don't know. These others always say, among other things, that my heart is in good shape. As if I didn't know that even without them. As if I didn't know about their hearts, even though I'm not a doctor. And I find it strange when they tell me that I'm lucky not to have sick tonsils, like most children. Because I'd swap illness for a problem any day. You just have to look at the special shoes I always wear to know that nothing is getting any better. At least not the way it did with Natalia's teeth after she wore braces for a year because they'd been a problem.

And so, for the first time I didn't go to school, and because of me, mum didn't go to the stall. I finally persuaded her that it wasn't a problem. "I can stay on my own," I said. I wasn't a baby. I was ten years old. Plus, I didn't want her to lose the only *shitty* job she has. Naturally, I didn't call it that. I was just repeating what she'd said about it. I don't think it's *shitty* to sell little cribs and little pine trees. Especially not if you believe in God. But if you don't, then that could be a problem.

When I told her that she could go to work, I never dreamt that I would cry afterwards. Before leaving, she said for the hundredth time that if I felt any worse, I should call her on her mobile since it wasn't there for decoration, it was so we could talk if a problem arose.

As soon as I heard the door close and the sound of her footsteps trail off down the stairs, I started to cry. That same moment I wanted to phone her and tell her to come back. I couldn't be on my own! I thought I could, but I couldn't. I was afraid of my hearing. I hear all sorts of things in the silence. The chair scraping, the cupboard breathing. The switched off lightbulbs fizzling. Not to mention the walls! They're made softer by the sounds on the other side. She left me a video of *Home Alone* so that I could see how much fun it could be to be home alone. I knew the movie by heart, and I knew that I wasn't finding it fun. It was a disaster. The mum in the movie hadn't really disappeared, she'd just forgotten her child at home. Which was worse than if she had disappeared. And on Christmas, to boot. She couldn't have chosen a worse time to be forgetful. I didn't think that even I could do something like that. And I'm famous for my poor memory.

But then I remembered that the owner of the stall (where mum always worked over the winter) was at our place the day before. He peeked into my room to see if I really was sick and had a fever. The truth was that I was in bed and could barely breathe. Mum said:

"Dammit, Igor, why would I lie? Listen to him – he's gasping for breath, like a fish out of water!"

It was true. That was exactly how I felt. Like a fish with a hook in my gill. It hurt a lot. Everything was sore and I could barely swallow my own saliva.

"Marina, listen, I'm really sorry..." Igor said when they'd closed the door to my room and they were alone in the hallway. "I'm fond of you, more than fond, but I'm not a welfare service. If I don't make money now, for the holidays, who knows if I ever will. What do you want from me? To pretend that I don't see that this is the fifth day in a row that you haven't been to work?"

"I just need another day or two. I can't leave him alone in this condition."

"You could get your sister over..."

"No, I can't. She and Emil don't get along. Anyway, I know she'd say no, and there's no way I'm going to humiliate myself and beg her..."

"What kind of person is it who won't jump in just once to help out her own sister? She must be a monster!""

"Don't call her names like that! The women in your family are no angels either, but, still, I don't call them names!"

"Alright, don't be so touchy! But can't you see my side? Do you know how much I have to pay that gang in the city council every month just to rent the stall? Do you know the competition I'm up against? Do you know how much one day of no sales costs me? I'll tell Maya to take over your job and that's that! End of story!"

His footsteps trailed off and I could hear the doorknob on the front door squeak as he turned it. Then I heard mum, in her soft slippers, quietly follow him out.

"Igor, wait, where are you going?! What end?"

She must have pulled him by the sleeve or something because his puff jacket, the kind that makes you look fatter than you are, swished loudly. For a while, there was silence while it spoke its swishing language.

Then I could hear mum sigh. And Igor cough. After that he said something that had nothing to do with mum's work at the stall. As if he was the hairdresser at the "Greta" salon where she had her hair cut.

"Marina! My beautiful little Marina. I've never seen a woman with such beautiful hair. It's silky and smells like… come closer so I can smell it again. Mmmm…"

"Stop it, Igor, that's enough! Let me go, I tell you!"

"Why should I let you go…where should I let you go… how should I let you go!"

"Emil is in his room, he hears everything, stop!" mum said quietly, fending him off.

"The two of us whispering at the end of the hallway? Marina, don't exaggerate…"

I strained my ears as hard as I could. But I wasn't up to it because I had a headache and a temperature. I thought to myself, who does he think he is, smelling my mum's hair?! Only I can do that! Doesn't he have a mum of his own? Let him go to her if he likes smelling something. I tried to get up and go out into the hallway to do I don't know what, but I couldn't. My legs were like two soft pieces of dough. And then I heard him speak again:

"Marina, listen to me, and listen good! There's a way for the two of us to reach a permanent agreement. You know what it is so stop fucking me around! I like you. I've always liked you. From the very start of our relationship…"

"Relationship? C'mon, get off it. The only relationship we have is a business one."

"You seem to be forgetting everything that's happened between us..."

"You're right: it happened! Once. And even that was an accident. If you ask me, the happening should be in the past perfect tense."

"Twice, we had...OK, let's call them happenings! I don't know about you, but for me you were no random choice. Actually, I'm very picky when it comes to women. And if your distance and coldness have something to do with my wife, I'm telling you, forget about her, pay no attention! I have nothing to do with her anymore. Except on paper. I've already told you, she's completely crazy and there'll soon be an end to it. Fuck it, court procedures take time. You've got to believe me..."

Then I again heard the jacket swishing followed by mumbling. Now, I don't know, maybe Igor wanted to smell her hair again, I often wanted to do that myself. But she's not always in the mood. She sometimes pushes me away, saying: "Emil, some other time, I've got to work now." I'm mentioning this because suddenly I heard, from way back in the hallway, a smack! A slap in the face! It was so loud that I froze in my bed, despite having a temperature of 38.5. At first, I didn't get who had slapped whom, until mum said:

"What do you think I am?! Get out of here! Go look for your fun somewhere else! I told you to stop!"

My heart sank, I was afraid that he would hit her back. But luckily he didn't!

"I'm not kidding, Marina, I'm serious when it comes to you..." he replied calmly, as if he had his finger on the page in *Catechism* where it says if somebody hits you turn the other cheek! If someone throws a stone at you, throw him a loaf of bread. In this case, it was: if someone slaps you, say something nice.

"Well then, we've got a serious situation here. I hope you understand and can accept it. I'll be at the stall tomorrow! I just need one more day!"

"And what do we do about your boy?"

"My boy, my worry!" mum retorted. "Emil will recover and I will work. I hope that this...this...slap doesn't mean...that I'm fired?"

"Marina, calm down, you know me, I'm always ready to come to an agreement. Especially with you. With you I'd do it till Judgement Day. You have no idea how beautiful you are, especially when you're angry, your cheeks flare up."

"Go to hell! You said what you had to say, why all this pathos now?!"

"You see, you really know nothing about me, you think that what you see standing here in front of you is a mass of muscles, a random pile of protein and that inside it's all hollow. Draughty. You've got no idea how wrong you are. But enough said. I've got work waiting for me too. So, we've agreed. One more day."

And so she wasn't fired. Even though for her, it was still a *shitty* job. Not a day went by without her telling me how she felt while doing it. Maybe she wasn't fired because the boss still liked her a lot. Because my mum really is very pretty and good, who wouldn't like somebody like that? I always notice how people in the street look at her. Women glance at her briefly, men look longer. Some even turn around. But that's not at all the same as when they see my shoes and turn around. When we're out in the street together, mum and I, she always looks as if she's holding a 10 by the hand.

Meaning: Emil with his bowed head + 0 as a kind of cloak of invisibility.

And so it was that I didn't recover as she had hoped after all. Which is why I'm here where I am.

I put down my mobile and tried to go to sleep. It didn't work. My eyes wouldn't close and I was hot. My ability to hear came of itself, not because I made an effort. Sounds came trickling in from all sides. They dripped like water from a broken tap. There were so many: footsteps, conversations, machines humming, more footsteps, parquets creaking, distant laughter, water in the pipes…

And there were also sounds from outside the window: magpies, sparrows, blue tit …the wind in the treetops. Suddenly I was surprised by the silence coming from Professor Antun's flat. I couldn't hear a thing. Nothing! And it was almost impossible not to hear him because he was just on the floor beneath us. He always had the radio on or was playing the piano. Then I remembered that I hadn't seen or heard him since that day in the park. Not once. And I was very attached to him. Especially since that last talk in the park. So, how could I have forgotten about him then?

I got up and put on my socks and slippers. I decided to go down to his flat, ring the doorbell and say: "Do you want to play the listening game?" Maybe he was sick and there was nobody there to help him. Mum had often mentioned an old people's home to him, because how long did he think he could continue living on his own? She jumped in to help him out as much as she could, but his needs were much bigger. "Marina," he would say, "let's get one thing straight, I'm not afraid of death, but you don't understand me, maybe you will when you're my age. To go to a home for dying is to inhale, morning, noon and night, the stench of deathbeds and wait to die, it's to do nothing except count the steps that separate me from the shadow of death. If you'd ever stepped foot in such a place, you'd know what I'm talking about."

I put on the top of my track suit over my pyjamas, opened the door of the flat and strained my ears. There was no one anywhere. I took the lift down to the first floor. It wasn't easy. My legs were too weak and I could barely move.

Even before I rang his doorbell, I somehow knew that the professor hadn't gone anywhere. He was there, on the other side, except there was a silence sitting in his chest. I understood: the two of us would never play the listening game again.

I rang the bell, though I don't know what exactly I expected. Who was supposed to open the door? Jesus? We'd learnt about him in our religious studies class. He created miracles when he wanted to. When he didn't want to, he made himself invisible. Angels? They were our invisible helpers too. But now the only one here was me, and I was extremely visible and helpless. I didn't even have a piece of wire to unlock the door and pretend to be Instantly. I kept pressing the doorbell until my finger went numb, I even called out to him a few times. I said I could clearly hear that I couldn't hear him at all anymore. I knew he was there on the other side of the door. I knew that he couldn't open it. But maybe he could hear me anyway, even if I couldn't hear him? Did he still have that special nose for people?

I took the lift back upstairs. To the flat. And then what happened? I went crazy like never before! I'd forgotten to take the key and the door was locked. In the meantime, after the *mishap* with the unlocked door, mum had changed the old lock for a new, better one. In other words, I couldn't even get to my mobile to phone her. Then I remembered Auntie Lilia. What would she say if she saw me trembling in my pyjamas, gaping at my locked door? Would she want to know how I solve a problem when I'm in a new, unfamiliar situation? You bet she would!

Well, the fact is I didn't solve it! That's to say, I solved it like this:

I sat down on the new carpet with its pattern of huge ladybugs and started to cry.

Naturally, *It's Good to Do Good* heard me. She had a nose for other people's problems, if I can put it that way. I've already mentioned that we live door to door. Wall to wall. This time she really did do good. She didn't do her usual boring hello and good morning. She must have seen herself that there was nothing good about my morning. She peered out from behind her door and looked at me in amazement for a minute:

"Emil! What are you doing here in your pyjamas? Where's your mother? Why aren't you in school?"

I didn't say anything, I just cried. How could I tell her everything? After sobbing all over my pyjamas, I eventually went into her flat. I sat down on the sofa while she made tea. Her old, orange cats started milling around my feet. I liked their warmth, attention and softness.

I answered her questions at random. I knew that it all looked stupid. It looked like that to me too. I talked about being ill, about the forgotten key and the dead professor, but I didn't know what I was saying aloud and what I was saying to myself.

"What professor?"

"Antun."

"The old man on the first floor?"

I nodded.

"When did he die? How come I didn't know about it? How come you know?"

"I heard."

"From whom?"

"From myself."

"Emil, don't talk nonsense! I'm asking you how you know that the professor has died?"

"I don't know how!" I said, still crying. Even if I knew, who would believe me?

She headed for the phone but before closing the door she said that she was going to call some people about what I had just told her.

I wanted mum! "I want my mum," I kept saying. "I want my mum!"

I wanted mum to kiss me, hug me, smooth the hair on my forehead. I wanted her to say "my specially produced little biscuit." But she wasn't there! I hugged myself and rocked side to side, calling out to her - to myself, then aloud, to myself, then aloud...

"Don't worry, darling, Auntie Vjeka will fix everything. Of course, we'll phone your mother. Her especially. We won't leave her out, I promise! Now lie down and get some sleep..."

Meanwhile, I started feeling very cold, even though Miss Vjeka said that it was warm in the flat. I wasn't warmed even by the saints, two Holy Virgins, several Jesuses and lots of angels looking down on me from the walls. *It's Good to*

Do Good was religious. Unlike mum. But I knew that my mum was a good person even if she didn't believe in God, but in…something else. In the brain. In the intelligence of the universe. But I was too young to understand what that was about.

My skin became more sensitive than ever, and I could feel it tingle all over. Everything hurt, everything bothered me. Even the blanket I used to cover myself. I almost vomited in this flat that didn't smell of mum or apple pie. In the end, I just fell asleep. But not before *It's Good to Do Good* shoved a little picture of a saint into my hand, saying I should pray because it would help me sleep. I don't know if that or something else was the reason, but I did fall asleep.

And when I woke up, there was another lady in the flat. *It's Good to Do Good* said:

"Emil, how are you feeling? Say hello to Miss Dunja. You're the reason she's here."

No way! I didn't want to say hello, I wanted mum. To say hello, you had to say *Good Morning,* and this was not a good morning for me. There was still no mum, no mum anywhere…

"Maaamaaa!!!" the word came rasping out of my mouth.

"Your mum will come, Emil, don't worry, right now she's busy," *It's Good to Do Good* leapt out of her chair and walked towards me with wide open arms, as if everything was just fine. If she thought for even a second that her arms could replace mum's, she was wrong! I jumped up just as she had from the chair and threw off the blanket. Holding the crumpled saint in my hand, I started crying out for mum even louder!

"It's alright, it's OK, I won't do anything to you, calm down...calm down," she kept saying.

I sat on the sofa and tried to smooth out the saint as much as possible. Though not much was possible. His face and robe were still crumpled. Whether because of the fever or something else, all sorts of ideas started coming into my head. Silly things. Things that had never occurred to me before.

Saints.

Why do they wear dresses, not trousers? How do you become a saint? How do you know you're a saint? Does a white circle appear above your head as proof!? You have magic powers and help the sick? Why aren't there more saints? What's the problem... I asked myself all this, the way mum asks when she comes to see what the problem is with my homework. Because my hands and feet need correcting. My thoughts were interrupted by *It's Good to Do Good:*

"You see, Emil, Miss Dunja just left. You didn't hear her say hello? No? How come? She said it loudly enough but you were deliberately fiddling around with that picture card in your hand and didn't want to tell her your name or what grade you're in! That should have been simple enough. I know you know that much. But I don't know why you wouldn't do your part. She only wishes you the best, Emil. That's all. You understand? No? She just wanted you to answer a few questions, but you kept on mumbling and staring at St. Anthony. (You don't say staring, you say praying!) Never mind, she'll have to have a talk with your mother. (Why?) That's how it is in her job. (What job?). Asking questions, sometimes uncomfortable ones, requiring honest answers." (I never lie!)

Anyway, what kind of job is it, I thought, if you have to answer questions to people you don't know? What's that got to do with mum and me?

"As for Professor Antun...I really don't know how, but you guessed correctly, Emil. You were completely right! The police broke into his apartment. The doctor says it was his heart. (Naturally.) I told the policeman about you, but he didn't believe a word of it. Imagine, he even said, Madam I didn't come here for fun and games. (I'm not having any fun either.) You can tell your fairy tales about children to somebody else. Anyway, in the end it turned out that you may have to make a statement, although, being the way you are, I don't know how a statement from you could help them check out information that has been proven to be correct. I tried to tell him how things are with you and that maybe it was all just a coincidence, that everything simply fell into place by the providence of God. I don't know how many times I told him what your real problems are and that, therefore, it would be better if I told him again what actually happened, but..."

And how am I? I wanted to ask her. How are things with me? Because I hadn't guessed anything regarding the professor. It's like mathematics, there's no guessing. You just know that's what it is, full stop. Except this isn't maths. And you don't use your head, you use...I don't know what exactly.

I didn't eat anything all morning. And I refused to drink anything. Mum didn't come, but I didn't know why. Auntie Zrinka appeared only later. She glanced in quickly from the door and said that she would be taking care of me now, which surprised me because mum says that *some* people (that's to say Auntie Zrinka!) only know how to take care of themselves. Because they can. Because they've had a stroke of good luck! And even that can sometimes pose a problem to them. The size of the stroke. I know, this sudden role of carer didn't make either her happy, or me. And so, without much talk, we went to our flat.

"I…don't…have the…key…or a piece of wire," I said, still worried about the locked door.

"What kind of wire?"

I had no idea how to explain what you do with a wire if you don't have the key.

"Look, as usual I don't understand you…"

She took a key out of her pocket, waved it in front of my nose and said:

"If this is what you were thinking of, it's called a key, not a wire. A wire is something completely different."

I know, I wanted to say, I'm not stupid, and you still don't know how to open a door without the key, but instead, I asked:

"Where's… mum?"

"Having an important conversation. Because, as usual, you messed up. Not for the first time. Instead of phoning her on the mobile, since you have one, no, you had to complicate your life and everybody else's to boot. So, until she returns, you will be with me, and don't even think of going out in your pyjamas again. Unless…you want to spend the day with Vjeka. In which case just tell me and we will go straight to the woman who was born to make decent people's life miserable with her various good deeds. Listen, she'd love that. As for me…I'm not going to argue with you. And I won't mollycoddle you either, like your mother, let's get that straight. So, let's hear it. Do you want us to go back?"

I shook my head really, really hard. Choose the lesser of two evils, as…I don't know who would say.

When we entered the flat, Auntie Zrinka made me a tea and gave me a syrup for my temperature. She spread butter and marmalade on a slice of bread and broke it into small pieces, the way I like it, the way mum does it. Maybe mum gave her instructions, because otherwise how would she know that everything had to be laid out on the little plate just so, along with the little blue Smurf toothpick to pierce the bites of food.

For a long time, neither of us said anything, the only sounds came from my munching because my nose was stuffed, and from her rustling the newspaper, which happens when you don't read and just leaf through the paper from left to right and back. Because your mind is on the movie playing in your head, not on the newspaper article. That's why.

But I preferred listening to the rustling of the newspaper than to the murmuring of her heart.

Mum

At first, I thought I was dreaming, because it was dark, and voices and shadows filled the room. The wind was sneaking in under the window, and I thought I heard mum's voice somewhere in the flat. I sat up and stretched my legs out on the bed. My hearing is never wrong, but this time I wasn't sure. Because, what if something happened like in the movie *Home Alone*? If it happened in the movie, it could happen in our flat. Which means, maybe she forgot me! And if that's what happened, for me, it couldn't be worse! A hundred times worse than if she had just disappeared on her own. Then again, maybe I was just dreaming about it all. Because in my dreams, even the impossible is possible. Like running or talking or laughing.

And then I thought: what if my hearing is on the blink? Because of the fever or something. Maybe it's gone rusty, like the radio in the kitchen that we don't play anymore, but didn't throw away because it's not ours, like the other things in the flat that aren't ours, that belong to the person who lent us the place. That's to say, rented it to us. Mum says that appliances and machines go on the blink and break down because they have an expiry date. Everything in the world has an expiry date. Even people! Especially their relationships. Everything, absolutely everything. So, I replied that God can't have an expiry date because otherwise he wouldn't be called eternal. And eternal means forever and since time immemorial. Something that has no beginning and no end. I read it in *Catechism*. It's like the circle in mathematics. If you draw it well and precisely enough, which I rarely manage, afterwards you've got no chance of knowing where you started and where you ended. It all becomes one.

I shouldn't have mentioned the word *mathematics,* because it immediately prompted her to ask:

"Since you mention mathematics, let's hear it, what is 16 minus 9?"

"?!"

First of all, we weren't talking about mathematics, we were talking about things that go on the blink and break down. Machines. People. Relationships. So, naturally, I said that I didn't know because it was hard for me to count when I had only ten fingers.

"You don't know, do you? But you do know how to philosophize about the eternity of circles. Well, you see, I've already told you that you need to make more of an effort with subjects that are important for you, but you don't listen to me at all! One day I'll get really angry and forbid you from going to religious studies class. Then we'll see who's the alpha and the omega of this house! Because you truly don't need to be brainwashed with more nonsense. You know?! You're really a genius at remembering only unimportant, irrelevant things."

God is unimportant and irrelevant? But I didn't want to argue with her. Number one: I don't know how to argue, and number two: people with quick tongues always win in the end. Actually, I do sometimes try to argue, but in my head. I find that in my case, soundless words are always quicker and more precise. So, I didn't say anything, I just thought that I wouldn't want the one subject I like in school taken away from me. The one subject that, unlike maths or natural and social sciences, I'm really good at.

That's what I was thinking as I walked to the room where the voices were coming from.

Now I was absolutely certain! One of the voices was mum's and the other was Auntie Zrinka's. I'd spent the whole incredibly long day with her, waiting for mum and looking out the window. I'd kept my nose glued to the window, waiting. I'd breathed on the glass and traced the words M U M. E M I L with my finger. Until Auntie Zrinka had told me to stop mucking around and making a mess, because when I finished somebody was going to have to clean that grubby window.

"Why don't you calm down and go to bed?"

"Because it's…daytime."

"So what? You're sick and you've got a temperature. You should be in bed, instead of sitting by the window. Your mum will be arriving any minute," she said again, even though I was calm. I wasn't crying and screaming like this morning, the only thing I was doing was breathing on the windowpane and tracing letters and hearts.

I stopped blowing on the windowpane. But I kept waiting for the sight of mum at the courtyard gate. I told myself that I would forgive her even if she'd forgotten about me, which was in itself un-for-giv-able! Just let her come back. But nothing happened. At least not while I was awake. I have no idea how I fell asleep. Maybe with my head on the windowsill. Maybe Auntie Zrinka later carried my sleeping body to my bed. I don't know. But it easily could have happened that way, And just as well that I didn't wake up at the wrong time to see it done. Darkness had fallen, that's to say, it had descended. Because darkness doesn't fall as quickly as people sometimes do when they fall un-conscience or as a stone does when you toss it into the water, when it falls slowly, imperceptibly, until it swallows up all of the daylight.

And then I remembered Jesus.

One evening he knocked at the door of his disciples, seated around the table. He told them that it was he, Jesus, that he had come to have supper with them, but Thomas replied that he didn't believe him, that he might be an imposter and that until he had poked his finger into his wounds, there would be no joint supper. This somewhat surprised Jesus, because he cared less about the food than about checking their faith, and if all the disciples were believers, then why was there a doubter in their midst? Jesus also said, "blessed are they that have not seen, and yet have believed." Like me. There are things I don't see, but I firmly believe. And I don't have to poke my nose or fingers or feet into what I hear under the surface in order to believe in them.

Mum's voice became clearer when I reached the door, although her whispering was softer than the night wind tangled in the treetop. I could hear Auntie Zrinka as well. Her voice was sharp and quick, it pricked the air like the needle on mum's sewing machine. I waited for a moment before going in.

Mum was talking about what had happened to her on the day that she'd disappeared. She'd spent the whole day explaining to someone what had happened to her, what had happened to me, and why it had happened to us. It wasn't her fault, she protested, because it can happen to any child that they forget to take the key when they leave the house.

She wanted to know who had reported her! They wouldn't tell her. She said that she knew anyway, she was sure who it was even if they wouldn't tell her. Nobody was as mean and obsessed with her private life as her next-door neighbour! The woman's own private life had gone wrong, naturally, so she lived off of somebody else's! Like a parasite!

"Calm down, madam," they told her, "it'll all be resolved, we are just acting on an anonymous call. That's our duty!"

"Did that anonymous call come from my building? From a woman who loves to brag about her good deeds?" Mum wouldn't let it go.

"Madam, we don't know what you're talking about. Calm down and answer our questions if you want to get out of here as soon as possible and see your son."

And so on and so forth...

She pulled herself up on the bed when she saw me standing barefoot at the half-open door. She was still wearing the same trousers and top as this morning, I'd noticed that she'd returned in the same clothes she'd been wearing when she disappeared. When somebody disappears, they always ask what the person was wearing. That's followed by a description of the clothes and their colour. Nobody asked me anything, but if they had, I would have been able to describe every detail of her clothes with my eyes closed.

She immediately opened her arms like the wings of a bird. As I went over to her, it flashed through my mind that there was nothing to forgive her for. Because she must have disappeared all on her own. That seemed to me to be the most natural explanation. Although it immediately reminded me of a movie. A science fiction movie. It's about a woman who vanishes, that's to say she falls into a parallel time. Like parallels in maths. Lines that lie side by side but never meet, and never will, they don't know of each other's existence. They just run on, like in that movie: the woman in one time, and her son in another. It's only at the end of the movie that the woman manages to return to the first parallel, but nobody believes that she was in another, people don't trust fantastical things; if they can't see it with the naked eye, for them it doesn't exist. Mum says my hearing is like that. And I say, OK, just without that science bit. Because it has nothing to do with science. It's plain fantastical. Because I'm like that. Plain Emil.

I didn't look at her even once, but I knew that Auntie Zrinka was watching us and that the expression on her face was like when you have something sour in your mouth. A slice of lemon. Or something like that.

Mum ran her fingers through my hair just the way I like it, from the back of my neck to the top of my head. She knows that I like it when her fingers touch my head like a gentle comb. I wouldn't let go of her even when she tried to pull me away because she had something important to say to me. Never more important than now, she said!

"Listen to me, tomorrow you will stay with Auntie Zrinka, OK? Just until you get better. I have to go to work. Say you're OK with it, Emil, that you won't be a problem. Look at me when I'm talking to you. Why that sad face now and that pouting mouth?"

I couldn't lie and tell her that I liked the idea. I whispered that if somebody had to take care of me, I'd rather it were Uncle Jakov. Auntie Zrinka let out a short laugh through her closed mouth. She'd heard me. I hadn't spoken softly enough. A bit of the laughter came out of her nose, and then she said:

"There, you see, I always turn out to be the mean sister, when all I am is realistic. Instead of smacking him or at least telling him off for all the things he's done, because he's incapable of understanding, you baby him, ask him, want him to agree. As for the other thing, what I said that he would say to you, he said it. I know your son better than you do! Didn't you say that he's not the problem, I am? If I changed my attitude, so would he…"

Mum broke in. "Emil!" she said, continuing as if she hadn't heard her. She held me away and again asked me to look at her. She brushed the hair off my forehead and kissed me. Once. Twice. Three times. Four times. A lot. Until I listened to her.

"It's very important for you to listen to me very closely now. If you keep being pig-headed, we're done for this time. Uncle Jakov can't take care of you. He's away. And even if he weren't, he's a busy man. Only Auntie Zrinka is free. There's nobody else I can leave you with. Tell me that you understand and that you agree. If you don't agree, I'll resign tomorrow. You know what that means?"

Not really. If I think that she still calls her job *shitty*, however you look at it. I know, though, that most of the jobs people do are all about money and numbers. And I'm not good at that. At the ab…stract. I'm only good at correctly hearing who loves me and who doesn't! Who would take care of me without a problem, and who wouldn't!

"How about Mikula, then? Would that be OK?"

"Mikula? How did you come up with Mikula? Of course it's not OK. Ever since he began doing the night shifts at the coffee bar, he's been drinking. He drinks at night, and sleeps it off during the day. Later he acts like a marathon runner in the park, thinking that nobody notices anything. Despite all that, his life style doesn't concern me, but he's no babysitter! Come on, Emil, be serious…"

I'm always serious so it's silly to say that I should try to be even more serious. The thing is, Auntie Zrinka and I don't get along the way I would certainly get along with Uncle Jakov or Mikula. I was just trying to help choose a good carer.

I nodded my head to show that I agreed with her bad suggestion, even though I didn't agree at all.

And then, as I was getting ready to get back into bed, mum suddenly heaved a deep, deep sigh.

And so I heard everything that came out of her after that sigh. Mostly crying. She'd cried before sometimes, but never like this. And they weren't ordinary tears, like mine or somebody else's, they were the opposite, they were invisible tears. Invisible because only the person they belonged to could submerge themselves in them. Nobody told me that, nobody explained it to me, I didn't read it anywhere, I reached that conclusion by myself. From what I'd heard. And I also concluded that mum certainly wouldn't want anybody to know about them. Especially not Auntie Zrinka. Because if she'd wanted that, then the tears would be visible. Auntie Lilia says that it's not nice to put people in an awkward situation, even your own mother. So, I didn't say anything. Even though I heard everything, which means that my fantastic hearing hadn't broken down one little bit.

I returned to my room and pulled the cover up to my chin. I gazed out at the clear, star-studded sky. I thought about the snow we wouldn't be having this winter. I thought about how it would take a miracle for snow to rustle down from the sky, and for a miracle I needed to pray to the saint under my pillow. I'd pray to him for…several things: for him to send snowflakes, for me not to have a problem with Auntie Zrinka tomorrow, for mum not to cry anymore, for me to recover my health…

We all have our own star. I read that somewhere. In a book, maybe, I don't know. And when you die, you go back…home. It's nice to think of stars as our real homes, not these borrowed homes we live in. If that's true, then Professor Antun has found his. Maybe he's looking down on me from such a star right now. He's too far away and I don't hear him anymore. Maybe he hears or sees me, because who knows how these things with people and stars work?

The wind is still sighing under the window. It's tousled the treetops the way mum sometimes does with my never-long-enough hair. I let it grow, and she keeps cutting it. It makes me cry, but she says: "It will grow back, what's all the fuss about, you're a boy, not a girl." Samson hid his strength in his hair. In *Catechism* it says that every person carries a hidden strength inside. He just has to find it. Where could mine be?

I heard a long branch scratch at my window, tapping like a crooked finger. I had a strange scratch at the back of my throat. Because of everything. Because of all the tears. Except I'm not like mum. When I cry, I can't fool anybody that nothing's wrong.

In the morning, I knew from the rays of sunlight streaming in from the top of the roller blind that I had slept late. Outside, the wind had abandoned the trees and they were now still. In the street, cars were buzzing around like bumblebees. In the kitchen, Auntie Zrinka was trying to find the station she wanted on the wonky radio, but naturally, she wasn't getting anywhere. Our relationship was like that. That's why I'd put off our meeting. So that there'd be as little static as possible. I pretended to be asleep every time she peeked in to check on me. She never once called me by my name, so I continued to keep my wakeful eyes tightly shut. I figured it was better that way. To pretend that I was asleep. I was somehow convinced that she was pretending too, pretending not to see that I was pretending. And it occurred to me that the only good thing we had was the way we both pretended.

While I was counting the little balls of light through my squinting eyes, I remembered a conversation she'd had with Uncle Jakov when I'd been curious and wanting to know what they talked about when mum wasn't around. I was watching the Smurfs on TV, so they didn't pay any attention to me. Since I don't talk, they probably thought I didn't hear either. It went more or less like this:

"I can't stand his silent staring, Jakov! That's the problem."

"You can't, well so what! You should see yourself in that kind of situation. You punish me for days with the same kind of hardcore silence!"

"What's that got to do with it? I'm not talking about us, I'm talking about him!"

"Look, people talk about themselves when they talk about others, let's be clear about that..."

"Stop philosophising! I wanted to say that I'm never sure what he really thinks."

"Hmm, to tell you the truth, after all these years I'm less and less sure what's going on your head. Maybe it's better that way. If people could read one another's minds, imagine the shit it would cause..."

"You don't understand, I wanted to say that, since he doesn't talk in the presence of other people, I'm never sure how much he understands, I maintain that healthy communication is a sign of intelligence..."

"Not wanting to talk and not being able to talk are not the same thing. Marina has spoken of a psychological block. Let's say, for instance, that you can talk but often won't, out of spite! What conclusion should I draw from that regarding your intelligence?"

"It's unbelievable how rude you are! Why are you picking on me? Lately you only seem interested in making nasty digs at me!"

"There's no need for that tone, I'm just saying that there is a thin line between these things and it has nothing to do with intelligence. You think that school grades are the only way to measure somebody's brain? A top grade of 5 in school is a measure of what? Intelligence or plain swotting! As for Emil, with him it's all about trust and being close. How close you manage to get to him. That's why I try to give him the space and time to realize that I wish him well and that I have become fond of him, that I like him just as he is, because he's special and different..."

"OK, what I care most about is my sister, even though I don't understand the things she's done with her life at all. Damn it, when I think of everything she's sacrificed! And for what? Have you noticed, because I have, that there's something strange about Emil's eyes? No? An uneasiness?

Nothing? You don't get the feeling that his eyes are somehow...scanning us?"

"I think that what bothers you is the feeling that you've got no control when you're around him, because that's what people like. To control. To oversee situations. To give others the best of oneself and hide the worst. In other words, people like to see the lay of the land, socially speaking. Which, in the case we're talking about, is not possible. Because it seems that at some deeper level, he understands us, but we don't understand him. And so it turns out that he's maybe stronger than we are, even if it seems to be the other way round. I mean, if you look at that body and that mind, which is almost locked like a code without a password. As for me, I gladly open my heart to him. You should do the same. I assure you, he feels it when someone is sincere when communicating..."

What does that mean, *scan...ning*? Everybody can tell you that I have ordinary eyes. I can't do anything special with them. Even when I close them, school doesn't vanish, however much I sometimes wish it would. They are as ordinary as ordinary can be, though mum says they are beautiful and quite big. They're the most distinct part of my face. Everything I know about eyes is written in Natalia's *Catechism.* The soul looks through the eyes like two windows looking out onto the world. Natalia's windows are blue like the sky. Mine are brown. Mum's are green.

I couldn't put off getting up anymore. And when I finally appeared at the kitchen door, it didn't occur to her to ask me ordinary things, the way mum does. For example: "Well hello there, where've you been, sleepyhead? Are you hungry? How do you feel? Why are you barefoot?" Instead, she started off with the one thing that always annoys me:

"Good morning, Emil."

I walked over to the table as if I was deaf and had forgotten my ears on my pillow. I didn't look at her, not once. Wouldn't want to scan her!

Her bracelets murmured and her earrings whinnied as she said:

"Say *aaaaah...*"

I swallowed a spoonful of syrup for my temperature. Then I ate some of the food she had made for me. There was nothing good about my morning, and I'm sure she felt the same way about hers. I thought about what the two of them had been talking about the previous night. I heard everything they said after I slipped into bed and gazed at the stars. Especially the things that were not meant for my ears.

Auntie Zrinka told mum that she had only herself to blame for the situation she found herself in. No, nobody else was to blame, just her! What was happening to her now was the consequence of past mistakes. What mistakes? Clearly, those when she should have gotten rid of me in time. (?!) Alright, she saw that the words "get rid of" were too strong, what she meant was some sort of institution for children like me. (?!) And yes, how many times did she have to tell her that she was stupid because she wasn't even asking the boy's father for child support. (!?)

The next day, in the afternoon, Natalia phoned. Mum answered. I never answer. Because mostly I just breathe into the receiver or answer any questions in my head, so you can't hear anything. Mum wrote down what I had to do for homework and said to her:

"Thank you, you're wonderful, what would I do without you."

In addition to maths, I had to make something out of modelling clay again. After she put down the receiver, mum burst out with: "Fucking hell, I'm sick of her modelling clay assignments!" This time, the teacher said, if I found it hard to work with the modelling clay, I could draw it with coloured pencils. Or I could write a few sentences. The topic was: "My mum!"

I was stunned! As if I ever found it hard to depict something with modelling clay? And especially not mum! I could do it with coloured pencils, of course, but I preferred modelling clay. I'd been practicing with it since kindergarten. It hadn't been easy at first, but now I'm very, very good at it. Maybe the best in my class, although the teacher claims that I never listen and show the wrong things.

Not true! She's got eyes, but doesn't see, as Professor Antun would say.

And while mum was hemming the dress of a woman who lives upstairs, I was standing at the window, looking down at the deserted courtyard. At the bare trees. At the birds with their fluffed-up feathers, looking like little feathery balls. Mum said I should do my homework, because I was going back to school tomorrow. I was healthy. I didn't have a temperature. I wasn't coughing. "Don't fool around, get down to work," she said in a way that reminded me that I'd never seen her cry. The way most people cry, when their face becomes bloated and their eyes get red. That's why she always looks the same on the outside. But on the inside? A flood! I told her that I was looking out the window because of my homework and was about to sit down and do it.

"So I'm outside? In the courtyard, am I?"

I nodded. Bullseye!

"Emil! Stop kidding around!"

I shook my head. Because I never kid around, I don't know how to kid around. And I didn't feel like explaining why I was looking out the window and where I exactly saw her down there, because it would take too long and could turn out that I was speaking nonsense. So, I didn't say anything.

I sat at the table because she kept staring at me. Her hands were purple and rough. And her nails were nothing like Auntie Zrinka's. She didn't use hand cream, because it made the needle in her hand slippery and the fabric greasy. And then what would she do? For sewing, you have to have clean, dry hands and good eyesight. And you have to have patience, especially if you're unstitching something and then resewing it. If you cut off more than you should, then forget it, says mum. It doesn't matter if you're yawning late into the night, a real seamstress keeps her word and finishes the work on time. In business it's important not to abuse someone's trust, she says.

I took the modelling clay and was done in a jiffy. This time I used mostly the blue, but also some brown for the rust and some grey for the ice. The two of us worked in silence, all you could hear were her scissors snipping at the fabric for the lady upstairs.

"What is…that?" she asked in astonishment when I said I was done. She had the same expression on her face as my teacher when she saw my butterflies, that's to say snowflakes. "I thought the topic was 'My Mum'!?"

I didn't say anything, waiting for her to recognize herself, I just continued to stare at my legs, which were as dry branches in winter. At the deformed soles of my feet, like curled dry leaves in the autumn. I looked like…actually, the crumpled saint under my pillow now looked like me. Except I still wasn't a saint. I didn't have the superpowers needed to correct everything that was wrong with me. I didn't look up even when she said: "Emil, look at me!" I didn't, and so what?! I was waiting for her to take a closer look at what I'd made. For her to recognize herself in it. Finally, she ran her fingers through my hair, the way I like it, as if combing it, and said:

"Alright. So that's me. An interesting metaphor! The fountain in our courtyard?"

She guessed right!

"Can you explain it to me? No? Alright. I won't insist. I have to say that you really depicted me nicely, even though I don't understand it. I'm surprised. Truly surprised! But don't you think that you've portrayed me…too abstractly? You know what I mean?"

"Aha. Like in mathematics…"

"You could put it that way. And you know that the teacher is not very good with symbols from the natural and social sciences. I'm guessing you'll barely get another poor grade 2, because there's no chance that a conventional little schoolteacher will ever understand this. But from now on, the two of us will stop worrying about grades, OK?" she said, tenderly planting a kiss on my forehead.

Not really, but I didn't say anything. What's wrong with, say, a top grade of 5? It's chubby and cheerful. Always smiling. As compared to a 1. Which is sad, with a hanging head. As if it's looking for its shoes on the floor. And a 2 doesn't look much better as far as its head is concerned. I put the clay model on the shelf, sat down on the sofa and reached for the remote. Just then the doorbell rang.

It was a real surprise to see Auntie Zrinka's face so soon again! I noticed right away that something was wrong. I mean, only yesterday, everything on her had been tip top. Every hair in place, as mum would say. Now when she took off her sunglasses her face was bloated and smeared with mascara. Naturally, that's what happens when you have visible tears. They're here so they can be talked about: why they happened, who caused them, and how to get rid of them as quickly as possible. Mum was beside herself and kept fussing over her, saying: "What happened?! Sit down! Tell me!" Before saying anything, and without looking at me, Auntie Zrinka pointed in my direction. Then they closed the door in my face, which was pretty silly. Because I become incredibly curious when there's a conversation going on that's not meant for my ears. It's an old story…

Auntie Zrinka and Uncle Jakov didn't have children, so I was surprised by what I heard.

If I understood it properly, Uncle Jakov was soon having a child with his secretary. (?!) Every so often, Auntie Zrinka called her a bitch or a secretary. (?!) To which mum said "disgraceful at one's place of work" (?!) Never mind that I didn't understand the words disgraceful and bitch, but it did occur to me that I was ten years old and still didn't know how children were made. And it's not that I didn't think or ask about it. Mum kept putting it off, saying that we still had lots of time to discuss it. Anyway, she claimed it wasn't important, she'd explain it to me one day. When I was more mature. There was still some time until then. I was lagging behind my peers in that respect anyway. So now I wondered: why was Uncle Jakov having a child with the secretary but didn't have any with Auntie Zrinka. How did mum have me? I know how caterpillars and worms do it. Some form cocoons, and some separate when they want to have young ones. Maybe it's the same with people, if there's no dad.

That day, Auntie Zrinka slept over at our place. I thought, OK, it's just one night. But…she prolonged her stay. As a result, I couldn't smell mum's hair when I wanted to, and mum didn't ask me to come and cuddle with her as she used to, nor did she call me her specially produced biscuit in front of Auntie Zrinka. She stayed with us, saying it was "temporary" and "until I figure out what to do." Mum disagreed. Their discussion went like this:

"I don't know what there is for you to figure out since you depend on him. Look at me, I don't answer to anyone for anything!"

"Don't be ridiculous. You don't really think that I envy you that kind of freedom, do you? I mean, you, my dear, are in a very, very unenviable situation, if we're being honest. You simply don't understand that you're teetering on the brink of existence, and now, goodness knows, on the brink of the law as well! As for freedom, that's open to discussion."

"And this from somebody who hasn't got a day's work in her employment record? I'm trying to imagine you working, say, at a stall, like me!"

"I think you've lost it a bit because of the situation you've got yourself into. What do you mean a stall! How can you imagine me in that semi-criminal world with those smugglers? You may have fallen that low, but I haven't. Don't be offended but, unlike you, I've been schooled for a job that's ten times better than hanging around stalls."

"As if I haven't. My education should also give me a better job than what I'm doing now. What planet do you live on, for God's sake? Mars? There are no jobs. And when there is one, I don't have the right connections to get it. There are up to two hundred applications to work as a cleaner in a state company. For the job of cleaning toilets and other people's shit you have to go through an interview with the employer and do a written test on the complete organization of the company. All that torture just for the job to go to somebody with better connections. I asked you only once to get Jakov to pull some strings, but you wouldn't help me..."

"Marina! I don't how many times we have to go over that! There were objective reasons why it was impossible to do anything at the time. His job was at stake, he was under scrutiny. All he needed was for somebody to dig up that he'd gotten his relative a job, for everything to go down the fucking drain!"

"OK, we won't argue about it. What happened, happened. It doesn't matter. In any case, I think that you should find a compromise with him."

I felt very sorry for Uncle Jakov. He phoned every day, but it was only mum who answered. "She's not at home," she'd say. "Zrinka's gone out," "Zrinka can't come to the phone right now," "Zrinka's asleep." I wanted to call him and tell him what was going on. They're here! They're talking! They're lying! But I didn't, because I wasn't sure I'd be able to speak. I might just breathe into the receiver and that wouldn't be good.

When Auntie Zrinka finally spoke to him on the phone, a torrent of words I had never heard before came pouring out of her mouth: moron, maniac, paedophile! The secretary he had a child with was twenty-five years his junior (apparently that's what it means to be a paedophile and a maniac). And what did he plan to do with that child now, she asked him. And the secretary?

It turned out that Uncle Jakov was going to acknowledge the child, whatever she thought about it (that's what it means to be a moron). It made her mad, sad, desperate. And that's what she told him: "I didn't know I'd married a moron. Even if we do get back together, that child will always be a stumbling block between us." (I don't know what that means.)

Personally, I think it's right to acknowledge what's yours. And guilt is something you acknowledge. In court. At the police station. In school when you forget your homework. It's not only good things that are ours, it's bad things too. I told mum what I thought about it. She told me to please apply my brain to more important things, like maths! And to stop asking about things that are not for someone my age. If I understood correctly, and I think I did, Uncle Jakov was not going to acknowledge the secretary (I don't know if that still makes him a maniac and paedophile). But I think that's what he'd decided. And one day when I came home from school, Auntie Zrinka was gone.

Two Hearts

MUM FELL un-conscience! I don't know how else to describe it except that out of the blue, nobody pushed her, she just fell to the ground. I have no idea why they say that. What does the word un-conscience mean, anyway? I only know the word conscience. Knowing right from wrong in the world, the world being everything that surrounds us: plants, animals, people, the sky, the sea...and sounds. So how can you collapse into something that doesn't exist? Something that doesn't belong to the world? Mum's legs suddenly turned as soft as two gum drops and they couldn't hold her up anymore. It all happened in the shop, by the till, between the Čunga Lunga chewing gum and the Animal World chocolate bars. I don't know what looked worse, her limp body lying there, although she seemed to have departed from it, or all those people touching her. Some of them lifted her legs up and splashed water on her face. I didn't do anything. I was paralysed with fear and screamed! I kept saying to myself: *Leave my mum alone, move away, don't touch her!*

A man raised a finger at me and threatened to pull me by the ears if I didn't stop screaming. It was piercing everybody's eardrums! She's not dead! She's just fallen un-conscience!

I shut up that instant. He didn't have to threaten me twice. When she finally opened her eyes, she sipped some water and asked what had happened. Naturally, I didn't manage to say anything. Everybody beat me to it, explaining what had happened. I clasped her and wanted us to get away as soon as possible from that un-conscience state she'd fallen into.

On our way out of the shop she tried to reassure me, as if I was the one who had collapsed into something impossible, not her.

"It's nothing, Emil. Why did you get so scared? It was stuffy inside, I didn't have breakfast, and so..."

"But it never happened to you before, you never fell un-conscience before."

"The word is unconscious. And yes, it did once happen to me before. But don't worry, everything is alright now."

Well, OK, I thought, un-conscience and unconscious, a few letters more or less doesn't change much.

On the way home, she carried a couple of big, overflowing shopping bags, but she wouldn't let me help her. She'd manage on her own, she said, they were too heavy for me. A load like that was not for hands like mine.

"And what are my hands like?" I wanted to know what she thought of them just as I once wanted to know if Mikula thought I was healthy even though I didn't do any running. I expected her to say they were problematic, but she surprised me:

"Artistic. What else would they be?"

"Look, we'll pop over to the pharmacy for a second," she said quickly, as if it had just occurred to her, and only because the shop with meds was right in front of us, on the corner, where we'd stopped so she could switch hands holding the heavy bags.

I started to rub my eyes, sniffle and trail behind. Because what if she fell un-conscience again? And everybody gathered around her again! And started touching her! Lifting her legs! And what if she didn't come out of that un-conscienceness? What then?

"Emil! Stop creating impossible scenarios in your head. Calm down. Why all this panic?"

I calmed down because the pharmacy shop is different from the food shop. Everything smelled nice. Everything was clean. It wasn't stuffy. The saleswomen wore white coats like doctors, but there was no way they were going to jab you with an injection. They didn't even handle money. As if, like me, they had trouble adding and subtracting. For that there was another saleswoman who wasn't in a white coat. So in the end, we came out of there faster than we went in. As we neared our building, there was *It's Good to Do Good* standing on her balcony. As soon as she saw us, she stopped watering the flowers and just stared at us. Mum pretended not to see her, and so I did the same thing. We didn't stop until we reached the letterboxes. Mum took out the key, removed the post and started flipping through it:

"It's always the same: bills, late payment reminders, ads. Pay this, pay that! Never a nice surprise or lucky win, so that the two of us could give ourselves a nice trip for once. Hah, what do you say to that?"

"You don't have…long nails."

"What don't I have?"

"Nails. Long. Like Auntie Zrinka."

"And what about them?"

"You buy a scratch card and scratch it. They say on TV that you can strike it lucky if you scratch it. So, it's better to have long nails."

I knew from the way she looked at me that I'd said something really stupid. But what could I do, that's exactly what I'd heard on TV. She didn't know anything about scratch cards because she didn't watch TV at that hour. She didn't watch it at any hour because she was always either sewing, or cleaning or cooking. However you looked at it, she was constantly counting her steps between the kitchen and the toilet. I'm usually in the armchair. It's old and the seat sags. It has cigarette burns on the armrests. But not because of me, because I don't smoke and I'm not heavy enough to make anything sag. It would be nice if I could, but I can't. When I sit down on it, the armchair shows no sign that I was even there. As if it knows that I look like the number 10. And I know perfectly well the sound it makes when an adult sits down on it. Before that happens, mum first covers the…disgrace, as she calls the armchair. She says she's disgusted by the furniture; the owner of the flat should have thrown it away, but he didn't, because he's a miser and pinches pennies wherever he can. There are always people like us (?!), to whom he can rent this lousy hole of a flat.

In the end, she found all this talk about scratch cards and nails very funny:

"What will you come up with next, Emil?! Do you know what else nails are good for? You don't? For instance, some people use them to scratch at other people's nerves and skin? But, you're right. Sooner or later you and I will scratch out a lucky strike for ourselves. There's no way we'll keep scratching out shit. It's not fair."

I nodded and climbed onto the wooden chair. I said that Miss Vjeka had received two copies of her magazine.

"How do you know there are two, eh?"

There was nothing for it, I had to admit what I'd been doing all these days, though I promised I wouldn't do it anymore.

"Well, if that's so, it means that she doesn't need this copy!" And instead of lecturing me about sticking my nose into other people's business, she pulled the extra copy out of Miss Vjeka's letterbox and we made our way to the lift. I wasn't sure if this was called theft, but I was pretty sure that Mr. Franjo would have said it was! Maybe he'd say: "Like mother, like son! Everything starts with what you learn at home!" Luckily, he wasn't around. I already had two or three diagnoses, according to him, and I didn't need any more. But then why did we take the magazine if we weren't thieves? As a joke? Yes, that's it, as a joke. Except I probably wouldn't understand anything in it and would laugh in all the wrong places. Or wouldn't laugh at all. Which was more likely.

"Maybe I'll wrap her *goodness* around the rubbish bin. Pity that Miss *Good-Doer* won't know what I think about her role as Miss Good Samaritan. Or maybe I'll think of something else. By the time we reach the second floor, something will come to me. Just wait for it. If only you knew, Emil, how lively and mischievous I was at your age. Unlike my exemplary sister..."

"You have another sister?"

"No. I have just one and her name is Zrinka!"

"I didn't know she was exemplary and good. You're better. You're the best."

"Oh Emil. It's just that the two of you don't understand each other. You're like two deaf telephones. And you don't give yourselves a chance to get to know each other better.

She doesn't have children, so her maternal feelings are stunted. And you don't have a brother or sister and don't understand how such relationships work. Fighting and making up are normal things. It's like saying *Good Afternoon* and *Goodbye* to someone."

She couldn't have picked a worse comparison!

"But Auntie Zrinka has a child now. That counts, even if it comes from the secretary, right?" I asked.

"Look at him! How on earth did you remember the details of gossip that isn't for your ears?! Well, the answer is yes and no. The child will never be hers, the little office flirt will use the child to blackmail them whenever she feels like it. You'll see."

I immediately switched to a subject that's always interested me.

"I'd love to have a brother or sister..."

"Emil, you want to discuss that in the lift now? Wait a minute, I just remembered something. When I was your age, I once threw pepper into the eyes of our neighbour's dog out of revenge. Did I ever tell you about that? No? You're not like me when it comes to character. You are my good little boy..."

I was speechless. Mum was worse than Tonko who kills animals, even if it's only in his stories. Poor dog. Maybe she blinded him? Who knows if he survived the pepper? I could hardly wait to hear the story. But I focussed on what interested me more:

"So, who am I like?" I thought this was the perfect moment for her to say the word "dad". For her to say: You're like your dad. Then I would ask: And where is my dad?

"Hmm, let's see. You're good-looking like me, you're good all on your own because I could comb through the whole family tree for such goodness and I still wouldn't find it, and as for your silence, that you get partially from Auntie Zrinka. OK, her silence isn't as extreme as yours, but not far from it. If we take into account that she uses it to manipulate and that it is part of her character, but not of yours. Let's say that she's one of those people who solves problems not by talking about them, but by keeping quiet about them. Then it becomes a matter of who gives in first. And in arguments it's the less talkative who win out, not the babblers knocking themselves out to prove something. But when Zrinka sets her mind on something, there's no stopping her. Unlike me, things have always happened haphazardly in my life. That's why I didn't finish university and she did. Your Auntie Zrinka graduated on time. She was the student of the year. With a straight A average."

"Why didn't you finish?"

"School you mean? Well, because you arrived...you. It wasn't planned. So, I had to decide very quickly between you and school. And it's clear what I chose. You see, my sister keeps rubbing my nose in it. The worst decision I ever made; she says. That's why Miss Perfection takes a dig at me every so often! So that I don't forget what I did to myself. But you see, even now, after all is said and done, I'd still make the same choice. Only, she can't understand that..."

I really didn't understand it. About the decision between school or me.

"And where would I be if you'd chosen school in the end?"

She raised her eyebrows, but this time she didn't look at me as if I'd asked another stupid question. She said, more to herself than to me:

"Well, my little man, sometimes you really do surprise me with your questions. Especially when I least expect them to be coming from you."

She took a breath, as if she was about to reveal the secret of where she'd be, when the lift creaked to a halt on the second floor and the iron door opened. And with it, the magic of our confidential talk somehow disappeared.

"We're here!" she said, and I hurried out after her.

Instead of going to our front door, she suddenly put the shopping bags down on the floor and started focussing on the magazine in her hand. If focussing is the right word for what followed, which was tearing and ripping it apart. It was as if she was destroying what was good, given its name. Because the magazine wouldn't have had that name if it didn't have good things in it. My legs turned to jelly. What would Miss Vjeka say? Mum handed me the key, told me to unlock the door, and without missing a beat continued tearing, crumpling and ripping up the pages of the magazine. As if it were hiding something. You could hear the paper tearing because there were no other sounds in the hallway. And in between all that, without raising her voice, she said:

"Hurry up with that door! Quickly! What are you gawking at? It's time we got rid of this rubbish…"

How was I supposed to put the key in the lock when my hand was trembling? Meanwhile, shreds of the magazine dropped to the floor like paper snow and the pile kept growing. When she finished, she gathered up the rest and dumped it in front of Miss Vjeka's front door. On the mat.

"There!" she said, as if she had done something wonderful, picking up the shopping bags from the floor.

"Mum? What's the matter?" I asked, the key still in my hand instead of in the lock.

"Quiet!"

"But mum..."

"Stop pestering! It's unbelievable how you always manage to get words out of your mouth at the wrong time and in the wrong place. Close your mouth and open the door. You want her to catch me?"

I got even more flustered. My hands cramped and I went rigid, especially as I could hear shuffling in Miss Vjeka's flat. She shuffled to the door in those message-printed slippers and stood there. You could hear breathing at the door. I mean I could hear it. Mum didn't hear a thing, so I pointed at the door. "Now what? A fault confessed is half redressed" I said aloud. "Stop with that religious fanaticism or else I'll take you out of religious studies forever!" she said in an irritated voice, although it had nothing to do with religious studies, it had to do with the teacher. I was just repeating what the teacher had said because I felt mum had been wrong to tear up the magazine.

But since I continued to just stand there all rigid, she put the shopping bags back down on the floor and shouted louder and more brutally than ever:

"You stupid clumsy boy! How can you be so clumsy-fisted? What's with the key! Give it to me!"

I can't say if I was angry, hurt or surprised. Maybe all three. So I answered in kind:

"I wish you would fall un-conscience again. And that somebody would throw pepper into your eyes!"

That really took her aback, so much so that she didn't manage to put the key in the lock either. And because I was angrier than I'd ever been before, smoke was almost coming out of my ears like that dragon in the cartoon, I kicked one of the shopping bags with my special shoe!

Boy did it explode!

The bag split open…

Everything came tumbling out and you could hear the tin of tuna roll down the stairs: bumpety-bumpety-bump… And everything else went all over the place. Naturally, what I'd said happened. *It's Good to Do Good* stood in her slippers in front of her wide-open door. In her place, I wouldn't have known where to look first either: at the pile of shredded paper on the mat or at the two of us, red in the face, standing in front of all the scattered things.

For a second, mum froze. And I froze even more. *It's Good to Do Good* asked:

"What's going on here, what's all this noise?"

"Mind your own business!" mum retorted as if the two of us had nothing to do with anything, least of all with the ripped-up magazine pages on her doormat. Mum hurriedly gathered up the scattered food.

"Emil, come and help me!" she said, because it was hard for her to gather everything up by herself, and things kept falling through the tear in the bag every time she tried to fill it. I pretended not to hear her. Although naturally I did hear her. I hear what nobody else alive hears, so of course I heard her! I didn't obey her because she'd called me stupid and clumsy-fisted. I couldn't stop thinking about the shreds of paper and the doormat. But *It's Good to Do Good* seemed not to notice. I mean, she didn't say anything. She just stepped over them and went over to mum. She bent down politely to help her gather up the various items. Picking up a little box, she said to her softly, her teeth flashing:

"Congratulations, Marina! You do these things so well, you're good at them! For you they're a breeze..."

"Take your paws off my things!" mum cried out, slapping the hand holding the box and making her drop it.

"Alright, don't be nervous. I just wanted to help. Seeing that Emil is, as usual, rooted to the spot, I just thought..."

"You leave my son alone! You understand! I've had it with your noble deeds and clever deductions about us."

It's Good to Do Good stood up, flailed her arms around as if fending off an invisible enemy and muttered that she had never wished anyone ill, least of all a child, because every child is basically a mirror of its parents, and everybody should think about the image of themselves that they wish to send out into the world. To which mum, straight off the bat, said that since she, Vjeka, didn't have children or, to put it colourfully, a mirror, where exactly was the reflection of her smarmy Samaritan goodness? Was it in poking her nose into the lives of other people's children? Or maybe in other people's mirrors?

A moment of terrible silence descended. That's to say, it was like what we sometimes get on TV – images but no sound. *It's Good to Do Good* headed back to her flat, leaving mum to barely gather up all the scattered items of food.

"Don't forget, the tenants' meeting is this evening at six, on the ground floor," our neighbour added, a second before we both entered our flat.

I just hope that she didn't hear mum's "fuck the tenants' association!" That it got lost in the slamming of the doors. My Smurf by the phone toppled over onto his back again.

I immediately threw myself onto my bed, I was so upset that I was trembling, while in the kitchen mum doubled over on the table. I crushed the picture of the saint under my pillow. It didn't look like anything anymore, crumpled as it was from wishful thinking. Unlike my loud sniffling, I could hear mum cry with invisible tears. But she didn't come to console me, so I waited for my tears to dry before getting up and going to the kitchen. She was still there, as if un-conscience, but sitting this time. She was full of water. Like the fountain in our courtyard. I could hear nicely. I don't mean the tears were nice, but as usual, I could hear them clearly. The table was still full of the things that had spilled out of the shopping bag. She was just holding the little box that *It's Good to Do Good* had picked up. She must have sensed I was there, because she looked up and beckoned me over.

It didn't take long for her to persuade me to come to her. Plus, she said a hundred times that she'd been silly, that she was really sorry she had said what she'd said to me. She would never, ever, ever say that to me again! Did I forgive her? *A fault confessed is half redressed*, I said…to myself. And hugged her tightly.

She didn't know what had come over her to behave like that, she said. Actually, she did know, but…

Just then, something strange and unusual happened. Something that had never happened before.

While we were hugging and cuddling, and she was running her fingers through my hair, I heard …two hearts or something like it inside her. One where it should be, in her chest, and the other in her tummy.

I waited for a minute to see if the sound would disappear, but it didn't. It was faint but it was there. I thought it was because I loved her. Or because she loved me. One of the two, or both together. When you love somebody, you hear their heart grow inside them. Then again, it occurred to me that maybe I'd only imagined it, though it's true that my hearing is never wrong. That's why I didn't want to say anything and spoil the peace we'd made or risk her saying: "Emil, don't be silly. What do you mean, two hearts?"

But I listened. Like a doctor using a stethoscope to listen to an illness in the body. Except I'm not a doctor and this wasn't an illness.

In the afternoon, mum went to the tenants' meeting on the ground floor after all, and without her in the house I was bored. I was supposed to do my homework, but I didn't feel like it. Given the choice of maths and the hallway, I chose the hallway. I could clearly hear them talking because their voices carried up the stairwell. They were all taking turns shouting like the kids in my class. Mr. Franjo, the tenants' representative, was the loudest:

"People are late with their payments for the cleaning woman and some bright sparks think that the lift will pay for itself!"

"And that applies to me, does it? I'm the only one who lives on the ground floor. Both physically and figuratively. Any way you look at it, I'm at the bottom! So, the people who use the lift should pay for it!" Mikula retorted defiantly.

"That's not how it works, comrade!" Mr. Franjo's voice boomed. "These are common areas and all of us have to pay for all of it."

"First of all, I'm not your comrade, you old commie! Your comrades are the people you robbed companies with, in your comradely way. You split it all up between you, from what I hear! Shares, bonuses, managers' salaries. The workers got zilch! So now, if you want to know the truth, I couldn't frigging care less about the lift!" Mikula answered back, after which there was the sound of a door slamming.

"Well, so much for culture and manners, my boy! And then you're surprised that you're unemployed. I love people who blame others for their misspent lives, and never take a look at themselves! Who'd want somebody aggressive and rude like that in their firm?"

"In which firm, Mr. Franjo? Nothing was left of the place where he worked after…after…" somebody spoke up in Mikula's defence.

"After what?"

"After the transition which was legal robbery. Let's be realistic," Mikula's defender said.

"Is that directed at me? Do you mean to say that I robbed someone?"

"Nooo. God forbid. I'm speaking generally. I don't know where you worked, Mr. Franjo, but I know Mikula's situation and what happened at his firm. The last twelve months' salaries weren't paid out. No wonder he's frustrated. A young man, with a university degree and no job. I hear that sometimes he wipes down the counters at neighbourhood cafés…"

"And so now what? I should shed a tear because of that? I've got my own problems that you know nothing about. This isn't a confessional and this meeting isn't called 'A Shoulder to Cry On!' What's wrong with working as a waiter? Is it shameful?"

"Well, no, but…"

"Listen, I'm not to blame for anybody's problems! I don't know who robbed the firm! The easiest thing is to look for a sacrificial lamb for one's own failures, and to find one in me. What's wrong with you people? Have you gone crazy? Let's proceed with the items on the agenda! We're talking about the front entrance and the outlays in our building, not about the state or social policy. You, Marina, will pay more for the water next month. That's to say, I'll count in an extra person. Now, you will ask me why."

"Yes. Why?"

It's Good to Do Good laughed, saying she never dreamt that word of mum's *good reputation* would travel so quickly and so far. Incredible!

"And I swear, I didn't say a word to anybody..." she added cheerfully.

"I don't know what you're talking about, Vjeka, but I'll come to you in a minute!" Mr. Franjo broke in, his voice serious. "You had a guest in the flat for three days, Marina. And you didn't declare her, but she was there, right?"

"Why don't you count twelve days for my sister? Are you out of your mind?"

"Sister or not, I don't care. And no, I'm not out of my mind. My mind works better than some young people's. And don't you start thinking about not paying, like this ruffian Mikula!" Mr. Franjo replied. Then Vjeka's voice piped up again, and then mum's, and again Vjeka's I couldn't catch all of it because they talked over each other, and then the other tenants joined in.

"Enough already!" Mr. Franjo roared. "Who's running the show here? Who is the representative?! As for you, Vjeka, don't assume that saintly pose when you talk. Your cats shed their fur all over the hallway, you haven't paid for the cleaning lady for the last two months, and you have people from prayer groups coming to you twice a week. About a dozen of them, if I counted correctly. And what are they doing in your flat? Just praying or are they also using your toilet?"

That, as mum would say, was the last straw. The ruckus that followed made it impossible to tell who was saying what to whom. I went back into our flat and turned on the TV. First came the Smurfs, and then: *Lotto: Your Christmas Scratch Card*!

I forgot all about my homework.

The next day, mum looked paler than the day before. I had less of an appetite than usual and just played with the food on my plate. She didn't eat anything. I wanted to smell her hair, but she said she wasn't in the mood. She didn't even look at my uneaten food, which was really unusual. She always made sure that I put at least something into my mouth. At least a small bite.

"Do you feel like telling me the story about the dog?" I asked.

"What dog?"

"The one whose eyes you threw pepper into."

"Oh that… Some other time, I don't feel like it now."

"I'm going to my room then, because you don't feel like anything."

"Oh, my sweetie-pie, come to your mum," she immediately said soothingly, opening wide her arms. "So much happened yesterday. I don't know how to explain it all to you…"

And so, we had barely started to cuddle when, within three short intervals, the phone rang. I could hear everything from the kitchen where I was crumbling tiny pieces of bread rolls.

Conversation number one:

"Yes? It's me, what can I do for you?"

"..."

"Well, Miss Dunja, you can come whenever you like. Who's stopping you from coming now, if you want."

"..."

"I assure you I'm not against it. We weren't home that day. You should have told me you were going to come."

"..."

"I'm saying that I'm not trying to avoid the law. Fine, it has to be a kind of surprise. What can I tell you? We were both in town. I have no reason to lie to you!"

"..."

"No! You can't get Emil on the phone because he doesn't talk to people he doesn't know, and communicating over the phone is yet another story. Yes! He has a mobile! I don't know who told you, but..."

"..."

"I repeat, I'm the only person he talks to, even on the mobile. It's as if you're very well-informed yet know nothing about him. And since you're so well-informed, why are you out to provoke me?"

"Alright. Agreed. Fine."

Conversation number two:

"Good thing you called. I was just about to phone you. I couldn't talk in front of everybody yesterday."

"Igor, be serious. That's not what I meant to say, I meant... I don't know why I'm even talking to you, maybe it's because we're in this together and I think the other side has a right to know. I don't know how to tell you. I'm still in a state of shock."

"..."

"Well, it would be nice if it had been out of love, but it wasn't. I had a pregnancy test this morning. It's positive."

"..."

"You're crazy. If I'd known you'd be happy about it, I wouldn't have told you."

"..."

"You can't come now. Emil is here."

"..."

"I don't need a hug. Please, stop. I won't change my mind."

"..."

"I'm not ungrateful. Of course I still need the job. It's just that I didn't want this."

"..."

"You mean to say you do?"

"..."

"This conversation is going pear-shaped."

"..."

Conversation number three:

"Are you still there? Hello? Zrinka? Why don't you say something?

"..."

"You're shocked? You think I'm not?! Look, it happened, and so what?"

"..."

"No! You're wrong! It was different when it happened with Emil but you can't understand that. Where did you get such ideas about him? I won't give him to anybody! And I don't care what you think! You don't understand anything about children. *His kind* are loved even more! You only know how to dole out untested prescriptions. You don't know anything about anything: not about children, not about people who work, and not about trying to make ends meet. The only thing you got right was...you married well!"

"..."

"Well, I'm sorry, you hurled the first stone. You crap on my way of life as if yours, along with all the money, is a bed of roses. And yes, of course, I'll say it again, what happened to me can happen to anybody. I mean, it happens to normal people..."

"..."

"OK, it can't happen to you for objective reasons. Forgive me. I really didn't mean for it to come out the way it sounded. No, I didn't mean it the way you say. You're taking my words out of context. And I'm not rubbing your nose in anything, because that's not in my character. Rubbing people's nose in things is your favourite sport. I was just confiding in you, as my sister. Who could I tell if not you?"

"..."

"No, this time I won't tell you who the father is! It doesn't matter."

"..."

"You matter to me. Everything else matters less."

"..."

"Alright, so...Hello? Zrinka, can you hear me? Are you still there? Hello?"

The Teacher

WHILE I was bed-ridden for a few days I missed out on some important things in school. Important because they were about the show, the allocation of roles in the school play, the recital and the songs. There was so much excitement: who would do this and who would do that. It looked to me as if I wouldn't be doing anything. But maybe that was just how it looked. Because things sometimes look one way and later turn out another. Whatever. Hanging up the Christmas and New Year's decorations made me happy and I thought about snow. If only it would snow, then everything would be perfect.

And then the same thing that had happened to mum, happened to the teacher.

At first, I didn't know what it was and why she looked different. On the outside she was the same. Her face and make-up hadn't changed. But there was something about the softer, slower way she was moving. So I just looked and listened, waiting for it to reveal itself. Because if it didn't reveal itself to me right away, it would do so later. That's how things always were with me.

Maybe I got on her nerves. Maybe it was like the problem I had with Auntie Zrinka. She told me several times that I should be looking not at her but at my notebook and doing the assignments she'd given us, adding that they weren't printed on her forehead or jumper or skirt. She knew, even when she turned around, that I was staring at her back.

I looked down. At my shoes, where else? Which didn't stop me from listening.

Our second lesson was art. The teacher told us to take out what we'd made with modelling clay and put it on our desks. I immediately noticed that Natalia had made a beautiful clay model of her mother. An added touch was the newborn baby cradled in her mum's arms. That's how we learnt that she wasn't an only child anymore. Now she had a brother. I saw Natalia look strangely at what I'd made. Still, she didn't say it was either pretty or ugly, just:

"I clearly explained to your mother what we had to make for our homework."

I didn't say anything. I wanted to say that there was no problem. I'd understood the assignment, but just then the teacher walked up to our desks. She praised Natalia's work in front of the whole class and said that the best Christmas present a family could receive was a brother or sister. And to portray it all so beautifully with modelling clay. I agreed with her. I wanted a brother or sister too. I just didn't know how it was done. Was it like with caterpillars or different somehow? I still didn't agree with the teacher on anything, but that was nothing new:

"Emil? Again? Can you please tell me what your piece is supposed to represent?"

"Mu…um."

"Mum? Really?"

"?!"

"Alright, then let's describe her. The way we just did with Natalia's piece! OK?"

No, it's not OK, I said to myself. Because she was already described in the piece itself. Why explain the explained?

That's not how it's done. Because I don't like it either when people use words to describe me, people like doctors, neighbours, the teacher, Tonko. Not in class. Not in the street. Not anywhere. Mostly they're wrong. And that leads to a confusion of opinions: what I'm like; what is and isn't wrong with me; what I can and can't do; what's best for me – a regular or a special school?

Everybody wants to prove that they're right, that their eyes see me better than anybody else's.

So, anyone who sees well will see mum in *my* piece and people who don't can't be helped! Even if you give them special glasses, they won't see anything.

"My mum is," she started, as if it was about her mum not mine. "…hmm…now what on earth is this supposed to be, Emil? A fountain? It's blue. And it's cracked in one place. No water is coming out of the fountain because it's rusty and old. In fact, there's no water because the fountain is broken. Isn't that right, Emil?" (laughter from the back row!)

I shook my head. As I said, we don't all have the same eyes for seeing. That's to say, ears for listening.

"You don't say?! And where am I wrong?"

"The water. Every…thing."

"Don't make me laugh, Emil…"

I shook my head. I didn't feel like laughing and I felt bad when she took words out of my mouth like that. She plucked them out. She made fun of me in front of the whole class. So that everybody could hear how stupid I was and how I hadn't understood the assignment!

"It…does… have…water," I said.

"Yes? And? What's with the water?"

"It can't…get out…"

"I still don't understand. Not to mention that the assignment was 'My Mum', it wasn't 'An Old Fountain'..."

And that's when something happened. Here. Inside. In me. Something snapped. It rang out like a dish dropped on the floor, shattering into a million pieces. Except I'm the only person who heard it. Which is why I couldn't stand either her or where I was sitting any longer. I plugged my ears and squeezed my eyes shut. As if my classroom, or at least I, could disappear. But I'm not so special that I can make it happen on its own, in front of everybody, so nothing happened. And I didn't go anywhere. My skin started tingling and I began to tremble. Which meant that I was just a step away from crying. And if that happened, everybody, but everybody was bound to see what was happening to me. Because, unlike mum, I didn't know how to cry any other way. To pretend that everything was OK when it wasn't. It was enough for me to start breathing rapidly and I'd be finished. Laughter could still be heard from the back row. I think the teacher finally understood that something unusual was happening with me. Because, when I didn't feel well, I hugged myself. And rocked left-and-right, left-and-right...

I heard her say:

"Alright, Emil, calm down, we won't talk about it anymore. And you back there, quiet!"

I waited for her to finally give me that grade of barely 2, so we could move on. But instead, she sat down on my bench. She sat so near to me that my ear was practically glued to her tummy. She'd never been that close.

Tapping her teeth with her pencil, she seemed to be thinking and trying to understand whether I was talking nonsense or there was something to it. And just then, while

I was looking at my shoes and slowly calming down, I suddenly heard the same thing in her that I'd heard in mum!

I was so shocked, so surprised that I stopped breathing because...I didn't like my teacher. I mean, it wasn't exactly that I didn't like her, but it was nothing like what I felt for mum. And it would never occur to me to smell her hair. Or let her run her fingers through my hair. That meant that I had somehow come to the wrong conclusion yesterday. Or had I? Maybe somebody else liked the teacher! Because I didn't really like her that much and that had nothing to do with me. I thought it was something else, I just didn't know what. Whatever it was, the sound was there. It rustled like snowflakes. Softly. Quietly. So beautifully that I completely forgot what had just happened and instead softly laughed out loud.

Loudly enough for the teacher to look at me. As if she realized, I didn't know how, that what I was laughing about had something to do with her, she said:

"What's so funny, Emil? Just a moment ago you were on the verge of tears. With all your pulmonary problems it's a good thing an ambulance wasn't called, and now you find something very funny? What is it? Does it have something to do with me?"

It did. But I didn't say anything. She didn't understand my blue piece. Or my butterflies. Or the white giant. So how could she understand this. Nobody would. Except mum. Though even she didn't always get it. And it wasn't as if I understood everything either, considering all those murmuring sounds coming from their bodies.

I wondered if either of them heard them. And if they did, did they hear them like me, or differently? Or not at all? Most people don't hear anything even if they have ears. I mean, they hear, but superficially...They're deaf to everything that's going on under the surface! Since I couldn't find the right word in my mouth and was afraid of another misunderstanding, I looked down and stared at my shoes. My ugly, special shoes. Even with my eyes closed, I knew where every fold was on their terribly shiny, smooth, undamaged leather. Because what could damage them? Taking small steps? Walking on the staircase when nobody was around? Looking at trees? Holding a ball? Running in my dreams? And as for those shoelaces! They hung limply without a sound to their name. Luckily, I suddenly remembered that I had that note in my schoolbag.

The note! I'd almost forgotten about it. I took it out and gave it to the teacher.

It said that mum gave Professor Nikola permission to do adapted physical exercises with me. The teacher stood up and spent a long time reading the note, as if I had given her a book to read, rather than a piece of paper. Mum's words were written there. How she'd met with Professor Nikola and they had agreed on the details of my physical education. If something wasn't clear, the teacher was free to talk to him.

"I didn't know your mother met with Professor Nikola. Why didn't anybody tell me? What are these arrangements being made behind my back?" she asked, looking up from the piece of paper. She did that with an even more questioning expression than when *It's Good to Do Good* asked me about Professor Antun's death. I wanted to tell her that the world wouldn't stop if she wasn't at the centre of everything. It wouldn't, and that was that. The world would continue to turn with or without her. Naturally, the idea wasn't mine.

I'd never have thought of it, it was mum's. But it somehow came to me now. By itself. It fitted perfectly! I could be clever too sometimes.

Alright, I didn't know she'd met with him either. She didn't tell me when that was. But she read out the piece of paper to me so that I'd know what it said. So that there'd be no surprises and I'd know. The teacher placed her elbows on the page of the grade book where my name was. And just when I thought she'd give me a low grade 2 again, she turned over the page and began to enter the grades for the others in the class.

The Swimming Pool

I'D FORGOTTEN about Instantly as if he'd never existed, but the day that the whole class visited the Natural History Museum, I ran into him again. The teacher said that there wasn't enough time to walk slowly to the Museum, so she would leave me in school because they would be back soon anyway. I kept saying that I wasn't a snail or a tortoise. I could go with them. I just couldn't run. And they wouldn't be running to the Museum anyway, would they? But I said it all to myself, so nobody heard me. She took me to the school library where somebody could keep an eye on me.

The librarian peered over her thick lenses and said, as if she had nothing better to do:

"I'm not paid for that and it's not in my job description, my dear, but I'll do it just this once," she agreed, not very enthusiastically.

"Emil, we won't be long, we'll be quick," the teacher said several times, as if that was the issue. Being quick. Since I wasn't going anywhere, I could slow down. I didn't care how long it would take them. And the fact that I wasn't going to see the museum or animals, who cared? And then she moved as if to hug me or something. You could hear clomp, clomp twice as I stepped back, leaving her arm suspended in the air, midway between the two of us. Maybe that's why something like a smile creased her face, though it was a bit sour. That's what you say when you don't know if the person is smiling or is serious, although I don't think she felt like smiling, and neither did I. Because I was crestfallen that I wouldn't be seeing the museum and the animals. Who'd feel like laughing in such a situation?

"Don't move from the library. Find something to amuse yourself with. Look through the picture books. Draw or something. You do understand that I have no choice? Perhaps some other time..."

No. That's to say, yes. I understood that she didn't understand me at all. But, as usual, I said nothing, I just stared at the floor, at the parquet, at my shoes, at my feet, at myself, at her, at...whatever my eyes landed on. Unlike talking, I had no problem with staring at people or things.

I don't know who wouldn't be bored after twenty minutes of leafing through a picture book. Plus, the library had no windows and I felt as if there was only dust to inhale. I told the librarian that I had to go to the toilet to pee. I wasn't lying, I never lie. I went, did my business, and then walked out the main door. I did not return to the librarian in the library. Because it didn't say anywhere that she had to take care of me. And it didn't say anywhere that I had to sit in the library with her. And if these things weren't written in...some kind of workbook, then you didn't have to do them? Well then, I wouldn't either.

I didn't go back for my jacket or schoolbag. All I could think about while I was walking was...the workbook and jobs. I felt all sorts of things, but I didn't feel cold. In fact, I was very hot as I tried to figure out how to get out of there and walk, walk, walk.... How to get as far away as possible from that stupid school...Everybody could tell from my face that I was as angry as...I wanted to say "a dog", but when did a dog get angry? Only people got angry. So it turned out that animals were better than people. Well, maybe they were. Anyway, I wasn't as good as a dog, and I was very, very angry! Most of all, at my feet! But not many people looked at my feet because given a choice between staring at my shoes or my face, everybody chose my shoes. I wasn't sure what conclusions could be drawn about me from that angle of observation. That I was special?

This is what I decided. I wasn't going home.

I walked farther, much farther, all the way to Uncle Jakov's and Auntie Zrinka's place. I didn't spend much time thinking about her because if I had, I'd have gone home that minute. But I didn't want to quit. I hoped that when I arrived and surprised them, she wouldn't be the one to open the door. I had chosen them as my destination, because I had no place else to go. I felt that I would manage somehow and that it would all work out in the end. I could have made it without a problem to the Natural History Museum as well, but I didn't.

I headed in the opposite direction.

Actually, I didn't know exactly where they lived. Or the name of their street. I knew I had to cross the bridge, then walk to the first intersection, and then further up to the second. That's where there were five big high-rises, all the same size, and two smaller ones. They stood there like five white whales with their two calves. I loved programmes about animals and I knew a lot about them, which was why I was so angry that they hadn't taken me with them to the museum. For instance, I knew that the calves of whales stayed with their mums all of their lives. They never parted. Never. Never. Never.

That's how I'm going to be. Like the calves, swimming next to…

"Hey! You idiot! Watch where you're going!!!" a driver yelled out of the open window of his car, furiously honking his horn as I crossed the street, thinking of whales!

I stepped back onto the pavement, but a wild stampede was thundering in my chest! A stampede is when a herd of animals runs together making the ground tremble. I was trembling too, repeating to myself: "Emil, stop having such silly thoughts! Look out when crossing the road!"

I knew I was close because I only had to go a bit farther along, by those white whales... . I mean high-rises! Their flat was somewhere nearby, I'd visited a few times with mum. As for the two of them, after that terrible row they had over the baby and the secretary, they'd made up. That happened in China. They'd recently returned from an exotic trip.

At first, when mum told me about it, I thought that it had happened at the Shina cinema, watching a film, with juice and popcorn. "So, what's exotic about that?" I asked her. I knew the word, because there are exotic fish, exotic cats, exotic birds, there are even exotic plants…But a cinema?

Mum immediately pulled out a map of the world and showed me China. The country is very far away and has a funny name, it sounds plates and cups. They sent us a postcard from a long wall that mum said could be seen from the Moon. I didn't tell her that I didn't believe it, just as she didn't believe that thing about Professor Antun and stars. She told me not to talk nonsense because people would laugh at me. I didn't want that, did I? It was impossible for somebody to see you from a star. (But it was possible to see the wall from the moon?) It was too far away. (And the wall wasn't?) Anyway, wasn't Professor Antun dead, she said. So how could he see me? Maybe I was absorbing too much nonsense from my religious studies class? The afterlife and crap like that...

So, since I didn't want her to start shouting again that she wouldn't let me attend my favourite subject anymore, I didn't say anything. Arguing isn't my strong suit anyway.

My uncle brought me a paper dragon from China that you let fly in the wind. Auntie Zrinka didn't bring me anything, but she didn't forget to ask if I was still going out into the street in my pyjamas? "Of course I'm not going out like that," I said to myself, "I never did!" As usual, my uncle immediately tried to shut her up.

"Zrinka, don't be mean. You really are tiresome. Leave the child alone and stop being angry at him. He hasn't done anything to you!"

"And he's not about to! That's not going to happen. If he were mine, I'd straighten him out. You'd see. But look at my sister, Jakov! It's her I'm talking about. A shit of a life..."

I thought that, like the last time, he'd say that when people talk about others they're really talking about themselves, because that would then mean that she had some shit in her own life. But he didn't. Maybe because they had only just patched things up and he didn't want more *shit*. Since we're mentioning that ugly word...

I didn't know what exactly she was referring to. Because I hadn't done anything, except that time when I fell ill, when I had the flu. But anybody can get sick. One day you're healthy and the next, who knows? I was healthy now. I wasn't coughing or sniffling. I didn't have a temperature.

It was just that I still couldn't run, though Mikula says that has nothing to do with health. Lots of people don't run, but they're still healthy. Like me.

My uncle promised he would take me out one day and show me how to fly the kite in the wind. As soon as the first proper northern wind came along, we would go out together and leave the women at home. That's what he said. Just the two of us. Like two men. Afterwards we'd stop off at a café and get something to drink. He still hadn't taken me, even though we'd had several northern winds. I always looked out of the window and watched the angel on top of the belfry turn its face to the north as the wind blew at its wings. I kept nagging mum about it, because I couldn't dial my uncle's phone number and breathlessly say into the receiver: "The wind is blowing. Let's go!" That's not how people make dates. People breathe and talk. I mostly breathe and say things to myself. Until finally mum said that right now my uncle was very busy with the new baby. He wasn't about to go out and chase kites with me. I shouldn't be so silly. That was just something people said: *we'll go one day.* I'd do better to accept that we'd probably never go.

And so, on my way there I started to feel a bit tired. Actually, I felt very tired! Halfway there I could barely lift my feet. It was as if somebody had put rocks in my shoes, that's how heavy they felt. And then, just when I thought I was close, that it couldn't be far away now, and that I wouldn't have to ask somebody to help me for the last stretch, Instantly suddenly appeared. He honked the horn of his Audi twice. His elbow jutting out of the window, he cried out:

"Well, well! I can't believe it! Who's that I see..."

I didn't say anything. He was all I needed on such a day.

"What is it? Don't you know me anymore? C'mon, don't pretend to be dumber than you are! Jump in!" He opened the back door of the Audi and beckoned me in. It was only when I was inside, sitting on the shiny, fragrant leather seat, that I realized how frozen and stiff I was. It felt good to be inside. Really good! As usual, it smelled of sweets.

Instantly looked at me, shaking his head in amazement. What now, I wondered. Where were we going? To the Supernova or somewhere else? I knew that he hadn't expected to see me here. OK, I hadn't expected to see me here either. Since I'd never been further than the kiosk, the rubbish bin or school.

"It must be fate that the two of us should meet when we weren't looking for each other, eh? Tell me, what are you doing so far away from home and school? I thought you couldn't walk more than ten steps on your own with those feet of yours.

"So...did I."

"What?"

"Think."

"Look, you surprised me. I've got a problem. Fuck it, that's how it is in my business; one problem after another. And the two of us aren't finished yet, we still have that little matter of your debt to settle. Which means that I don't have to drive you around town like a prince for you to finish your job. You can do it on your own. I've learned in this job that I can get the most from the people I least expect it of (and he pointed at me). And zilch from the most capable. They screw me. They use their intelligence to think up ways to screw Instantly. You understand? So, tell me, where've you been these last few days? I hung around your house and school a bit…Where were you? Were you sick? The flu is going around…"

I nodded.

"And now you're OK?"

I nodded a few times to show that there was no question about my health. Because that's what Mikula thought too. But I didn't want to mention him, or the running or being fit, because he would certainly say: "Who's Mikula? Running? What are you talking about? You shitting me again?"

"So why aren't you in school?"

"Because I'm not …in the museum."

"What museum?"

"Of na-tur-al-his-tory."

"OK. More crap. Like that time with the rubbish. I ask you one thing and you answer another. Fuck it. But when you're given a job to do, you're great. I mean, you're made for this work. Once you pay off your debt, you can continue doing it if you want. You want some pocket money? No? Why not? Anyway, now that we've run into each other, what about doing a little job for me?"

I didn't say anything. I gazed out the window. It didn't mean yes and it didn't mean no. It meant; I don't know.

"You ever been up to the swimming pool? No? Some kids like you go there to swim. Wanna go and see them?"

We came to a huge building that could have come straight out of a science fiction movie. Huge panes of glass covered the length of the walls, so you could see everything inside. And inside there was lots of steam from the heat. I knew how to swim and I wasn't afraid of water, but I never come here because it's a problem for mum. Because of the car we don't have. I was barely listening to Instantly's story about the job he had for me, when I noticed none other than Professor Nikola standing by the pool! In shorts and a short-sleeved top, as if it were summer, instructing the kids in the pool. A whistle hung from his neck.

"What's the matter?" I suddenly heard Instantly ask. "Are you even listening to what I'm saying?"

"?!"

"Do you hear what I'm asking you?"

"I'm hungry...," I said the first thing that came to mind. And it was partly true because I'd left my donut in my schoolbag and was tired from all that walking. I felt a little nauseous. Maybe because I was hungry. I wasn't sure. Probably it was a bit of everything. That's what mum sometimes said: "Emil, I'm a bit sick of everything."

"Hungry? How come right now? Lucky you don't feel like taking a piss. OK, what do you want me to get you? Tell me..."

A little further on was a stand with chestnuts and popcorn.

"No problem!"

He soon came back with a big box of popcorn and handed it to me along with a new little white packet:

"Take this. The client is at the back of the pool, by the empty offices."

"I don't have...a pocket."

"You don't have what?

"A pocket."

"Where's your jacket? Where did you leave it?"

"In the library."

"???"

He was thinking. About the pocket or the library. Who knew? We weren't doing very well with all the questions and answers. He looked me up and down, eying my shoes. And then I remembered and said:

"In the popcorn."

"Huh?"!

It took him only a second to realize what I was saying. And then he burst out with:

"Brilliant! Great camouflage. Who would suspect a disabled person with a box of popcorn? You'd have to be really retarded to think of something so perverse."

This time the client was a woman. Instantly described her like this: long hair, long legs, long nails, long eyelashes, the woman was waiting for her child to finish his practice session, and was slightly nervous so she was chain smoking, but he, Instantly, didn't like working with nervous people because then they made him nervous, plus he was having problems with some bad people and he didn't want them to see him, so I was a much better bet, always stable and calm, like that time at Supernova, I'd be great, he had confidence in me.

Nobody had ever told me before that they had confidence in me, but…

…I didn't feel like stepping out of the warm car into the cold, with just the popcorn in my hand. Long, grey clouds were gathering up there above me. That was a good sign. Of snowflakes.

Nikola

I WAITED, but the client didn't show up at the designated place. There was nobody around the empty office space. Just lots of dust, rubbish and broken glass that cracked under my special shoes. Everywhere you looked there was... ugh, shit! And a bird with a fixed stare! I had to watch out where I stepped. I had to take care not to look at that bird whose dead stare seemed to be following me. The place stank of...all sorts of things. I stuck my nose under my top and breathed out of my mouth as if breathing my own self.

I don't know. Maybe I didn't wait long enough, or maybe the woman wasn't coming anyway. The point is, I didn't feel like waiting anymore. It was cold. The popcorn in the box became as hard as little white stones. OK, I wouldn't have eaten it even if it had been warm and soft. I don't like popcorn. Of all the silly stuff (that's what mum calls sweets, chewing gum, popcorn and chocolate) the only thing I eat are soft gum drops. I walked toward the entrance to the pool because I'd decided, since I was already there, to say hello to Professor Nikola. Just briefly. For five minutes. I'd wave, that's all.

Inside I was greeted by a pleasant warmth, lots of voices, laughter and the splashing of water. Some grown-ups were waiting at the entrance door, but Professor Nikola was still standing by the pool in his flip flops, as if it were summer. I wanted to walk in, because he couldn't see me from where I was standing, but I came up against an obstacle. A metal bar blocked my way. I bent down and slipped under it. But in the process, I spilled some of the popcorn and when I tried to gather it all up, even more spilled out. Maybe half the box. There was now quite a lot of popcorn on the floor. Just then, a woman in a cubicle that I hadn't noticed before spotted me.

"Kid! You can't bring food inside! Do you even have a wristband to come in?"

Wristband? Food? I shook my head because all I was holding was the popcorn and the small packet for the client. Mum says that popcorn isn't food, it's just recreation for teeth.

"Are you here with your parents?" she asked suspiciously, standing up to get a better look at me.

Again, I shook my head.

"So, you're here on your own? Your parents don't know?"

Correct. But the last thing I wanted was to chat with her about how I happened to be here without mum. It would take a long time, and maybe she wouldn't have understood me in the end anyway. No, she certainly wouldn't!

"What's your name?" She wasn't just suspicious; she was curious too.

As if I'd tell her! I mean, what did she care what my name was. I'd just come to say hello to Professor Nikola, that's all. Why such introductions when I didn't care what her name was, and I wasn't planning to ask her.

"Well, since you won't answer the question," she said, raising her voice, "gather up all the popcorn you spilled, each and every piece, and leave! If you want to come in, you either have to have a wristband or be accompanied by your parents. There's no third choice. If you give me a hard time, I'll call the police. Get going, beat it!"

I didn't budge and just listened to her mention the police as if I had done who knows what! Eh, Tonko would have had something to say to her if he were in my place! Because I didn't care about the pool, even though I would have liked to take a dip, I just wanted to say hello to Professor Nikola. That's all.

"Did you hear what I said? Are you deaf? Move away from the control panel! This minute!"

I certainly wasn't deaf, but my hands were terribly sweaty from the heat. It felt as if the box in my hand was about to disintegrate. And imagine the mess all that popcorn would make. Plus, there was the packet at the bottom of the box. In the end, the woman stepped out of her cubicle and started walking towards me. I saw her raise her hands! She was getting closer and closer! And…

I couldn't move so I sat down on the floor! Actually, I was so tired and scared that I collapsed! And that's when everything finally spilled out of the box. The popcorn, but, by some miracle, not the packet which was stuck to the bottom of the box. Naturally, this was followed by tears. I cried longer and louder than I had in *It's Good to Do Good*'s flat. Even so, the woman still didn't understand that she absolutely shouldn't touch me!

But she did! She tugged me by the sleeve and pulled me up!

That's when I bit her! I bit her finger, although I'd never done that before to anybody!

By now quite a lot of people had gathered around us. The woman screamed that I was crazy, that I'd bit her like a rabid dog, that I should be ashamed of myself, biting at my age. I saw that some of the popcorn was very wet, so I started picking them up one by one. I had to put everything back in the box. I guess somebody called the cleaning lady because she now appeared with a broom:

"Leave it, boy. I'll sweep it all up and toss it in the rubbish. Come on now, calm down, it'll be alright"

No, it won't! I started to really scream, pointing at the box. I was hoping she'd realize that I wanted every single popcorn back. Every single one!!!

But she didn't. Because she started sweeping them up, and I continued to scream and grab them from under her broom. And then! Professor Nikola appeared. Thank God! I know, I must have looked awful, with all that snivel coming out of my nose and mouth. And there were hairs from the broom on my hands. The popcorn looked horrible. Like trampled snow in the street. He ordered everybody to step away from me and told the cleaning lady to put my popcorn back into the box. Right now! Never mind why! Now!

"I know the boy, he's a pupil of mine!" he said, taking me under his wing. "He'll be with me!" And that's how, after all that trouble, wiping the tears and everything else away with my sleeve because I had nothing else, I finally made it to the other side of the iron bar. But not to the pool.

"You can't go any farther in your shoes. You can only go in barefoot, in flip flops, having first washed your feet. That's why they wouldn't let you in. But tell me, Emil, what are you doing here?"

It would have taken me a long time to answer that, if I'd only known where to begin. While I was trying to think of the right words, he asked another question:

"Aren't you supposed to be in school? Where's your teacher?"

"At the museum."

"The museum? You mean they went to the museum, and left you at…"

"At the library."

"You mean the classroom?"

"The library."

"Never mind. How did you get here?"

"On my own."

"Incredible. I'm surprised."

"Me too."

He laughed and said that he didn't know I could be funny when I wanted to be. Like that time in class when the teacher got so mad, though she shouldn't have because Professor Nikola knew that I hadn't meant anything bad. I hadn't, had I, he asked. I shook my head. Of course not. I never wished anyone anything bad. I only once said that thing to mum about throwing pepper in her eyes, but I was immediately sorry. It was great to have somebody say I was funny because nobody had ever said that to me before. Though I wasn't quite sure what had been funny about it. I'd only been telling the truth. And the truth can't be funny like lying or telling jokes.

Sometimes, when I look at smiling faces, I notice that some people smile only with their mouths. The rest of their face is as stiff as my legs. On Professor Nikola's face everything smiled. Especially his eyes.

"Wait for me ten minutes while I get dressed and I'll drive you to school. OK?"

At that moment, I could have done anything and everything with Professor Nikola. Wait. Walk. Laugh. Be serious. I could easily imagine him as a dad. It would be great to have a dad with a face and smile like his! And all those muscles and all that goodness. For the first time, I wished that I had somebody else, apart from just mum, run their fingers through my hair.

I thought intensely a few times about his hand - my hair, but nothing happened. Nothing. It was only the wind that lifted my hair. Professor Nikola's hands were busy with the car keys. And that was that. End of story.

Return

PROFESSOR NIKOLA'S Mini Morris was neither big nor comfortable, and it had no particular smell. The seats weren't leather, they were made of some sort of pale fabric and were slightly frayed. But I didn't really mind. The only thing I minded was the danger of seeing Instantly. What would he do? What would I do? What about the popcorn? But he was nowhere to be seen. He'd vanished, just like the client. Professor Nikola kept real sweets in his car and said I could help myself. They weren't gum drops. I didn't take any. I didn't like peppermint.

"Sit here up front if you want, just put on the safety belt," he said as we got into the car, as I was about to squeeze myself into the back seat. Naturally, I immediately accepted his offer. Because I'm not a baby! I'm ten years old. But I didn't let him help me with the safety belt because I wanted him to see that I could do it by myself, though it took a while for him to explain and for me to understand what went where. Until it clicked. First in my brain, and then in the slot for the buckle.

"You're old enough to observe the world from the front seat," he said and off we went.

We quickly arrived at the school. Already waiting for us were mum, the teacher, the librarian, the director of the school and a policeman. The teacher was the first to open her mouth to say something, but mum raised her hand and stopped her:

"Not a peep out of you! Enough! Nobody could get a word in edgeways with you. We've listened to all your excuses and mention of special schools! Just so you know, we're not finished! In fact, we've only just begun!"

Oh, what a long, warm hug we had. Along with a few kisses. And fingers running through my hair. Luckily, mum didn't ask me anything, because I had no idea where I'd start. Maybe from the end. That was nicer than the beginning. She held me for a long time. Then we both breathed together. I into her, she into me.

"I went…you…know…to the pool…by myself…myself," I whispered into her ear so that nobody could hear me, though that was silly. Everybody knew already. It wasn't a secret anymore; the only unknown was how I'd managed it.

"I know everything, everything. Nikola told me," she whispered into my ear. "So I immediately calmed down and came to the school to wait for you. I was out of my mind when they called to say you'd disappeared. How, I asked them? Tell me what happened to my Emil."

"What do you mean Professor Nikola told you?" I asked, surprised.

"What do I mean? Why, he phoned. Home. How else?"

"How did he know our number?"

"Is that the most important thing in the whole story right now? I'll explain when we get home."

Home, or some other time, that's what she says when she winds up not telling me anything. If I waited for that story the way I did for the one about the dog and the pepper, I'd have a long wait. It went like this: the librarian fell ill when she realized I'd gone. She was a woman of a certain age, had high blood pressure and a weak heart. The ambulance came, but she was alright now. She'd calmed down. "It's not at all her fault," mum said.

"Of course it isn't," I replied. Her workbook doesn't say that she has to take care of me."

Mum opened wide her eyes in surprise and asked:

"Sorry? Where did you hear something like that?"

I waved it off and thought: never mind, I'll explain it to you when we get home.

"And you know what else I said to them? Do you know, Emil?" she immediately said.

I shook my head. How would I know? I wasn't there when they were looking for me.

"I told them, if you don't find him this minute, one of you is going to disappear too. Swallowed up by the night!"

"Like in the movies or in my room?" I wanted to ask. That's what they say in crime films. And the next thing you know, there are dead people in the movie. That's what being swallowed up by the night means in the movies. The darkness slowly swallows them up. And everything looks as if it's disappearing although I know that it's here, that it exists. It just seems invisible to the naked eye. All you can see are some shadows making creaking, breathing, cracking sounds.

But that wasn't important now, something else was.

I'd clearly heard mum call Professor Nikola by his first name. Without saying "Professor". She addressed him like a friend, but for my teacher she still used the formal form of address. When did they become friends? When did they exchange phone numbers? Nobody told me anything. OK, I knew that the world wasn't going to stop if I wasn't at the centre of the story. But, still, I wanted to know. Because if

I noticed something between the two of them, you can be sure my teacher did too. She didn't miss a thing when he was in question. As soon as somebody mentioned his name, there was a loud beating in her chest! She wasn't going to like this. She wasn't going to like it one bit!

Taking my coat and schoolbag, mum said:

"What's that filthy, squelched popcorn in your hand?! Throw it away!"

I held it even tighter and shook my head! That surprised her because I didn't usually eat popcorn. She tried to wrestle it out of my hand, but I clutched it to my body and let out a loud – NO!

"Marina!" Professor Nikola jumped in (No "Miss"!) "He wouldn't let go of the popcorn even at the pool. Let him be. (Surely he should be using the formal form of address?) It doesn't matter. Let me give the two of you a lift home. Emil is exhausted and freezing."

She quickly agreed, and so did I. Because I felt exactly the way he said.

"You know what I keep thinking?" he said to mum as we walked towards his Mini. "How did he do it? I simply don't understand how he managed it? Maybe it was to teach everybody a lesson, to show who he is and what he can do!"

I didn't think I had done anything special. It just happened that way. By itself. Who knew how it would turn out some other time? I was so tired I couldn't think anymore. And so we made our way out. Everybody else had already started leaving. The librarian slipped her bag onto her shoulder, waved at me, blew a kiss and went off. The policeman closed his notepad and stepped into his car. The school director was one of the first to vanish because, he said, the important thing was that nothing had happened to me so there was no need to make a fuss, we shouldn't let a little incident like that ruin the school's reputation. It was only my teacher who stood there alone, to the side, staring. I was staring too. I think our stares were directed at the same thing: Professor Nikola's hand on mum's back.

Mum kept thanking him.

"Thank you a thousand times over! I'll never forget what you've done. How can I ever repay you?"

"With lunch!" was Professor Nikola's ready reply, as if his hunger was hanging out of his mouth and he could hardly wait for her to ask. "I hear that you're a good cook and that your cakes are finger-licking good."

Nobody paid any attention to my teacher anymore. Nobody except me saw her reach for the wall. As if her legs had turned into gum drops like mine. And it didn't seem impossible that she might collapse into her own un-conscience world right there, in the middle of the school hallway, among the hangers and cupboards.

In the course of the next few days, several things changed in school. I couldn't say if it was for the better or worse. But I knew that nothing was the same as before. My teacher stopped being angry at me. She didn't ask for my homework. She didn't say: "Emil, think with your head, not with your hands." I wasn't of concern to her. For her, I had become… transparent. She looked straight through me. Even when my mind wandered, she didn't bring me back from that *other film* playing in my head.

And mum?

I was waiting for her to say something about my teacher. I was waiting for her to tell me how to behave in class if the teacher said this or that to me, the way she usually did. I was waiting for her to say something, anything, but she didn't. She stopped mentioning her. For her my teacher had become transparent too.

And the best days of the year were approaching, according to my religious studies teacher. And I agreed. This is what happened to me in the classroom.

During a lesson, she whispered to me that I could get a straight 5 from her if mum let me attend religious studies *for real*. She didn't pester me too much about it, just a little, then she wanted to know who my dad was. I looked down and thought about this mystery that was bothering her as much as me.

"Because every child has a dad, so why haven't you? That column in the roster is blank ..." She went on, with me still staring at the floor, as if he, dad, was hiding somewhere under my shoes, that she had never seen anything as beautiful as the cribs I had made out of modelling clay. I had magic hands and that was a true God-given gift. She showed them to everybody in the parish. What was more, I could write down all of God's commandments without making a mistake. I was a good and obedient child. She'd never had a better pupil. But could I somehow persuade mum to let me join the religious studies class for real next term? Not like now. Then I'd still have time to make my first Communion! It was never too late.

"And your mum, what about hers? I shrugged my shoulders. I honestly had no idea what having a first Communion meant. I mean, maybe we had it somewhere in the house, in the cupboard or drawer, I just didn't know that was what it was called.

Also, I was really happy that mum, along with a few other parents, had accepted the teacher's invitation to the *Help Our School show* – that's what the piece of paper I brought home said.

"Of course," mum said without giving it much thought, as if nothing special had happened between the two of them. "No problem. I can sew the costumes with my eyes closed. Now tell me, sweetie-pie," she said, "what are you going to be in the play? A snowflake or a butterfly?"

Lunch

HER MOBILE started getting a shower of text messages. I like that word – shower. It has a swishy sound to it. The *sh* slips out between the teeth and the lips. It's like hearing the rain falling. Like drops on the windowpane. Like the sound of sparrows and pigeons splashing around in puddles left by the rain, until the seagulls come and chase them away. When they drink water, the other birds each wait for their turn. That's the kind of bird they are, they're like Tonko. Sometimes they're not thirsty at all, but they still stand firmly in the puddle, staring down the other birds, gauging their fear.

Sometimes I would see his name light up on her phone. But never with the word "professor" attached to it. Sometimes, if her phone rang in her hand or her bag, I would try and guess who it was. I liked playing the listening game, especially since I'd stopped playing it with Professor Antun. I played it on my own now. I was good at guessing who it was. The noise in her chest gave it away. Or the silence.

And then that lunch happened. This is how it went:

She sat me down at the table, looked me in the eye and asked if I would mind if she invited him. "Who?" I asked, although I knew perfectly well who she meant. She just shook her head and said:

"Why the pretence? As if you don't know. Who's the best professor in the school? Who wants you to do PE? Who has the best muscles? Who is the *bestest*? I want to somehow repay your...rescuer."

Surely I was the one who should repay him? It's me he rescued, not her. But alright. I didn't know how to cook or thank him in some other way. It could turn out badly, like that time with the mobile. Maybe it's better to leave such things to her. I nodded in agreement but I didn't admit to her that she was getting on my nerves. I think it's only natural that it sometimes happens with one's nerves. And she got on my nerves because she had been planning it without me for days. Because she hadn't explained how they had become friends. And because she thought that I didn't notice how many text messages he sent her every day, and she sent him (more than ten)! But most of all because she knew in advance that I would say yes. I admit, more than once I imagined him being my father, because he was a good man and had all those muscles, but as far as I was concerned that's all it was. My imagination. His fingers running through my hair and all that...none of it happened even though I once thought it would. I didn't exactly know what she was imagining but it clearly didn't stop there. Considering the lunch that was going to take place.

"During lunch, we'll decide on your exercises for PE. We'll see about getting a pair of trainers," she said, from which I deduced that the lunch was a good idea. It wasn't just about her; it was about me as well. But I was always afraid of surprises. Because who knew what could happen in the end? Things start off looking one way and can turn out differently.

The aroma of the roast cooking in the oven wafted through the flat. Mum also made my favourite apple pie. I'd been unusually excited from the moment I woke up that morning, I was incapable of playing with anything other than the strap on my slippers. The sound it made calmed me. I kept yanking it off and pressing it back on, off and on…

She was gripped by a different kind of excitement. I'd never seen her like that before. OK, Professor Nikola was coming, so what?! OK, she liked him, so what? I liked him too, but that didn't mean I couldn't like him still more. As if he were my dad. Or a friend. Or at least somebody like Instantly. So, I didn't know why she was so excited and anxious, as if she might make a mistake in cooking, the way I could make a mistake…in anything. Anyway, she wasn't the one getting ready for PE, I was. A decision was about to be taken about the first trainers in my life, not hers!

And then, at one o'clock, the doorbell rang! *Driiiing…*

"Marina, you look wonderful!" he said at the door, giving her a bouquet of flowers as if it were his heart wrapped in the fragrance of roses. He was right. Regarding the way mum looked. She was wearing a dress I had never seen before and jewellery that she only took out for special occasions. As for him, he looked better than usual too. He smelled nice. The top he was wearing had never been tighter. And all those muscles underneath! Who knows what I looked like to them? Nobody commented on how I looked. Maybe I looked the way I usually look. Nothing special.

"Good afternoon, Emil, how are you?" he said, finally noticing me and giving me a chocolate bar.

Number 1 - let it be known that I'm not quite clear about greetings. What do you say if you're not having a good afternoon or day? And if you are, what about it? Or what if you don't yet know what the day will be like, because you've only just got up and smelled the morning, listened to it, and now somebody is telling you that it's a good morning and asking you at the wrong time how you are? How do you answer that? How should I be today? I'm always like me. Like Emil. I'm not very good at explaining what it's like being me. Because it's hard to describe others, let alone oneself. So, I didn't say anything and I think it looked as if I didn't know the answer to his question. Which wasn't far from the truth, because I wasn't sure. We still had to see how I would be.

I glued my eyes to the floor. I knew every squiggle on the tiles and every hole in the parquet of our flat. Depending on where I happened to be when people dropped in and would ask me something. I didn't look up or hold out my hand to take the chocolate. Although I saw myself doing it in my mind. My hand stayed clenched behind my back, like my tongue between my teeth. And so, as usual, mum did it all for me. She took the present and said: "Thank you, you shouldn't have..."

And then, as we walked to the kitchen, she poked me in the back a few times, signalling me with her eyes.

And I knew what that meant. But all that poking and eyeballing didn't help. That never got me to talk. And it didn't this time, either. That was not the way to push words out of my mouth. It either happened or it didn't. Full stop. I knew that welcoming him without saying anything was stupid on my part, since I'd been forming and practising sentences for this moment all day. I'd even written some of them down. And some I remembered. But, as usual, I let everybody down.

Mum was furious...the way mum can be sometimes! Her tone turned cold and she stopped talking to me...with her heart. It went like this: when we sat down at the table, she put up a wall between me and them. Like in a science fiction movie where you could erect an invisible wall so that whoever was on the other side couldn't see or hear you. That's what it was like here. She continued to talk to Professor Nikola as if nothing was wrong and there was no wall. I simply did not exist in their conversation. Nobody mentioned any trainers. She didn't even tell me to finish my meal, the way she usually did. She let the wall rise up to the ceiling and beyond, she let my food go cold until a thick film of grease formed over the soup. And how was I supposed to eat that then?

"So, you're not hungry? Alright," the invisible wall suddenly came down and she took my plate into the kitchen. It was the same with the meat. After she cut it up into small pieces for me, the invisible wall suddenly rose up to the light on the ceiling. So, what could I do except move the morsels of food from left to right, or to the rim of the plate, or hide them under the crust of bread. I managed to take some of the pieces of meat out of my mouth and put them in my pocket without anybody seeing. I could toss them into the rubbish bin or toilet later. And I was good at hiding bits of food that refused to go down my throat. Like a hamster, I'd collect food in my cheek, without swallowing it. That's how my words were now, like big morsels in my cheeks. They were waiting for something to happen so that they could come out. Because you never knew what might propel them. In the end, mum called me into the kitchen to help with the dessert. And there she quietly exploded:

"What on earth's the matter with you?!"

I shrugged my shoulders.

"Why are you behaving like this?"

I shrugged again. She went on, saying that she thought I'd like having him here. Had she known, she wouldn't have invited him! And later I'd say that others were the problem? Was that what I'd say?

I shook my head.

"Pull yourself together and look inside yourself, at the problem you have with people!"

How, I asked myself? How do you look inside yourself? I was better at listening to what was inside others.

I wanted to justify myself, but she raised her finger.

"This is neither the time nor the place for excuses. We're going back to the living room. Try to make amends. Nobody's going to bite you if you open your mouth and say a few words. Any words. You know yourself that Professor Nikola understands you. That he is fond of you. When he sees you, he says, he sees his younger brother who is just like you. He lives in another city now, so they don't see each other that often, but he misses him terribly. You understand?"

"What grade is his brother in?"

"He's already a grown-up."

"A grown-up? Where does he live? With his mother?"

She was quiet for a moment, until she finally said:

"I don't know. Stop asking irrelevant questions. We're talking about you now, not him. I'm trying to tell you something else..."

"I'm staying with you forever. I'm not going to live in another city when I grow up. If the calves of whales stay with their mums all their lives, then so can I. I saw it on TV..."

"Emil, stop! What whales?! What's the matter with you? You couldn't have chosen a worse time for your crazy ideas.

Take the slices of pie and watch your step," she said, quickly shutting my mouth as we walked to the room with our hands full. I carried the plates carefully to the table and put them down, afraid of being not just tongue-tied but clumsy too. And then we'd have to pick everything up off the floor. Meanwhile, she poured the coffee for the two of them. Then Professor Nikola asked:

"You're quiet, Emil. Did I bring you the wrong chocolate or is it something else?"

I didn't say anything, I just kept mashing the pie with my spoon until it was impossible to tell the difference between the biscuit and the apple. I decided to pretend not to have heard the question because who knew what was wrong with me or how to explain it? Naturally, the chocolate had nothing to do with it. Though it would have been easier if it had, because then I could say: "I like the one with rice, not this one with hazelnuts. That's the problem - the kind of chocolate. Bring another one so we can start to talk."

That's how Tonko might answer.

But what could I say?

And so I was preparing to ignore his question and ask him about PE and the trainers. Because either they'd forgotten why we were all there, or I'd got something wrong.

"Nobody made you angry, did they? Surely, not me! Just say so, if I did..."

I shook my head.

And then, just when I thought I had a sentence waiting on the tip of my tongue, he asked:

"Do you maybe have a problem with your teacher, Emil?"

Sorry? What's my teacher got to do with anything? I quickly shook my head.

"Are things OK with her now? Is everything alright?"

As my thoughts shifted from the trainers to my teacher, my tongue miraculously loosened up. I decided to finally boast about....what I was best at.

"Things with her are...great," I said.

"Really?" they both smiled in amusement, as if by agreement. Although I hadn't said anything funny, I hadn't even tried to be funny. "Can you explain the word great to us? If it's not a secret..." Professor Nikola said, asking yet another question.

I shrugged my shoulders because that same moment I realized that I had made a mistake. That I shouldn't have said anything. But the two of them looked at me like nosy old bags, as mum would say. The way they looked at me glued me to my seat and I started sweating, waving my arms and head in the hope that they'd leave me alone. I rose from my chair, planning to go, because I didn't feel like sitting or talking or listening or eating anymore, but mum thought differently:

"Wait! Who said you could get up from the table? That's rude! First answer the question, then you can go!" she said, pushing me back onto my chair.

So, I said what I had to say, because I had no choice.

After that we sat in silence for a while, the kind where they say you can hear a pin drop. But nothing was dropping now. Instead of words, it was as if I had poured concrete into the room. And there was nothing to be done about it because now we were all up to our neck in it. Although the room still smelled of coffee and apple pie, everything seemed to be steeped in concrete. The first to speak was Professor Nikola. He laboured to pull his words out of the soft concrete:

"What...do...you...mean...two hearts?"

"Simple. One is...here (I pointed to my chest), and the other is...here (I pointed to my tummy). There are two."

"Who can hear something like that, Emil!"

"I can."

"But that's impossible!" he said, looking at mum, waiting for her to agree. But she didn't do anything, except flutter inside, flutter her eyes and listen to me flutteringly.

And then, while he was pondering the possible and the impossible, I was saved at the last moment by suddenly remembering Instantly's popcorn. I had kept it hidden in the room for days. I kept changing its hiding place in case mum thought of throwing it away. The last hiding place was at the back of the wardrobe in the bottom box that had held Mikula's trainers which he used for running in the park. I hadn't checked for a few days if the popcorn was still there, so I decided to do it now. I asked mum if I could go to my room. I'd said what I had to say. She nodded her head and asked Professor Nikola if he'd like some more coffee. He didn't care anymore. He didn't say it aloud, but I could see. Anyway, you could hear it in his chest. That he didn't care.

He scratched the tablecloth with his fingernail, squelched the crumbs of bread and said: "No thank you, Marina, I've had enough." Mum didn't take her eyes off him. I didn't take my eyes off her. He didn't take his eyes off me.

When I closed the door to my room, they continued talking. I stopped listening because I had more important things to do. I opened the wardrobe, then the shoebox, and then all the other boxes! I took them all out and opened them one by one! Not a trace of anything! No popcorn anywhere! Just a single shrivelled piece at the bottom of

Mikula's shoebox, to prove that once upon a time there'd been a whole boxful! For a second, I thought that maybe they'd all gone for a run around the park, along with Mikula. Except for the shrivelled one which didn't manage to go with the others. How could it, considering the shape it was in? But, of course, they hadn't gone. I wasn't so stupid as to think that popcorn could run. It was just something that had flashed through my mind. Naturally, mum had thrown them away! What else could it be? My heart was pounding so loudly that I thought the other two would hear it in the kitchen. If they tried hard enough. But for the time being they were trying something that had nothing to do with me. I wasn't at the centre of their attention anymore. And that was good. Because just thinking of Instantly made me break out into a cold sweat. He would talk about "debts" again and say: "You know how much that costs?"

I didn't know! I barely knew the price of a lollipop. I reckoned that, after this, I'd be paying back my debts for the rest of my life. I didn't know how, but I felt that I finally had to tell mum about everything. Only where to begin? From the end?

Soon I heard Professor Nikola thanking mum for lunch and the apple pie. He knocked and opened my door, saying: "Emil, goodbye. See you in school."

Thank God I managed to wave and smile at him. At least something good for the end. *See you*, I said to myself, and went back to looking unhappily at the empty shoeboxes.

"We'll be in touch, Marina. We have to talk, alone. I'll explain everything. Now's not the time. Thanks again for the lunch," he said, pulling on his jacket in the hallway.

As soon as he closed the door behind him, I came out of my room with the box and asked about my popcorn.

"Honestly, what next?..." is all she said, rolling her eyes on her way to the kitchen. I went after her and repeated what I'd said, only a little louder this time. In case she hadn't heard me the first time.

"After everything you did at lunch today, or more precisely didn't do, you think you've got a right to ask me for some answers? So, now we're talking about that rubbish you didn't eat and hid for days in the dustiest corners of your room? Is that it? Of all the hobbies in the world, you had to choose collecting shoeboxes and the leftovers of stale food you don't even like? Just to be clear, that's out of the question and I won't allow it! You want mice breeding in the flat? Honestly, I don't know what you're up to, but just so you know, I threw the popcorn away two days ago. If you want popcorn, I'll buy you some fresh popcorn, but you're not going to hide it in your room. As for the boxes, you've got enough. There's no room in the wardrobe for any more!"

Hey! That very minute I threw myself onto the floor and started screaming! I hurled the shoebox into the air. I told her that naturally this was now a disaster and that she didn't understand a thing. Not a thing! Least of all, how much it cost!

"What? The popcorn? Don't be silly. Anyway, there's nothing for me to understand except that you went beyond the pale today!" she said, after which I only screamed louder. And then, for the first and last time in my life, she slapped me. Afterwards she called it a little slap, but I still called it a slap-and-a-half! We simply couldn't agree on how hard that slap was or wasn't.

"There, it's nothing terrible, just enough to give you a reason to cry," she said. "Now go to your room and cry till tomorrow! But first, clean up your room and tidy up those boxes, or else they might wind up in the rubbish bin like the popcorn!"

I cried and then some! I cried as I gathered up the shoe-boxes and smelled them, imagining that I was running away from mum, from home, from school in the shoes that had once been in those boxes, and later I cried with my head on the pillow. Until I fell asleep.

She came to my room late in the afternoon. I woke up just in time to see the object in my room disappear into the shadows of the night. When she sat down, the bed groaned under her weight.

"Emil, listen to me. Please don't pull a face like that, as if I did who knows what to you. Nothing happened that you didn't deserve. Now listen, I talked to the social worker the other day. I know you don't know what the word means so I'll try to explain it to you. It's the profession of that woman, Dunja is her name, I think you once met her at Vjeka's flat. It's her job to check if I am or am not a good mum. If it's good for you to be with me or not. If it might be better for you maybe to be somewhere else. She can separate us if she decides..."

"You're not good!" I said, still angry, clasping my face where she'd slapped me. "You threw away my popcorn! You won't let me collect boxes!"

"Don't exaggerate. I'll buy you fresh popcorn. Right now, if you want. But, alright, I'll give in on the boxes. You can keep piling them up in your wardrobe. But try to be serious from now on. You're not little anymore. You're ten years old. Instead of helping me, you're making things difficult. You want Vjeka to hear us arguing through these thin walls? You think I need yet another report against me on top of the one of child neglect? There'll be people who'll think I'm some crazy woman who beats you up every day. If somebody wants to do me harm, and there are those just waiting for such a chance, they can turn my every word around. That at least is easy these days. A slap in the face or on the bum, and right away it's child abuse. It happened and now I regret it. But let's get back to today's lunch."

"Your pie came out well..."

"Let's forget the pie. I haven't come to sit next to you and talk about food. Listen, how many times do I have to tell you to keep your gift to yourself...you know what I mean? And why wasn't I the first person you came to with that story about the teacher? Instead, you had to brag about it in front of Professor Nikola! You always tell me about how nature breathes, how snow falls, how a cat walks - alright you didn't tell me what the connection is between the fountain and me, but I know you will one day – so, why didn't you tell me about this? The two hearts? Huh? You're not saying anything...Emil, we agreed, you can't say such things in front of people who don't know you well enough."

"Professor Nikola...knows me."

"Not well enough! Nobody will ever know you the way I know you. What do you want people to think of you? As if what they already think isn't enough! Surely, you must feel that your mum loves you, despite everything. There's nobody on earth I could love more than you! They could even take you away somewhere, somewhere where they think you'd do better than being with me, but still, nobody will ever love you the way I do. The rules of the heart have nothing to do with the points of law that people who administer justice like to refer to."

My eyes welled up with tears because what she said was so beautiful and so sad. I didn't know what to say. But I didn't have to say anything because we immediately kissed and hugged each other so, so tightly. And I decided that this evening I wouldn't think about either Instantly or popcorn.

That's when I thought of first communion. I asked her if she knew what it was.

"What made you think of that now! Of course I know. Why do you ask?"

"You had it?"

She thought for a minute as if she couldn't remember where she had put it. Finally, she said: "Yes, why such a question?"

"It's not me asking, it's the religion teacher who wants to know."

"Sorry? How dare she?! That nosy old bag..." but she didn't finish because this time I was quicker:

"She said I should persuade you to let me go to religious studies for real next term! It's my best subject. I'd get a 5. Mum, imagine, the top grade, a 5!"

"I'm imagining that next time I'm going to give her a piece of my mind! It turns out that I keep having to go to school to argue with somebody! I know now that it was stupid of me to agree to let you sit in on her lessons with your class. You're all ears for the wrong subject, Emil. And you have no ears for maths!"

Her hair was all over the place and it smelled so good. It was soft, like the silk nightgown in her drawer which

I sometimes open and smell when she's not around. The room completely disappeared and the objects in it sank into nothingness. And just when I was about to ask her if she kept her first communion in a drawer, and what it looked like, and was it her First Story from when she was a child like me, she beat me to it and said:

"Emil, rest your head on my tummy."

I immediately obeyed and hugged her.

"Tell me what you hear."

Trainers

"If Tonko's going to be a writer, what am I going to be?" I asked mum after she had sent me to throw out the rubbish twice in one day. She simply wouldn't understand that I didn't like throwing it out at all! First of all, it stank. And second, somebody might make fun of me. That hadn't happened yet, but you never know. Somebody might see me and then it could become very funny. They were already making fun of me for all sorts of reasons, I didn't need another one. It was obvious from her answer that she didn't understand at all what I wanted to say.

"I don't know, Emil, you'll find something. Every person has a talent for something. Now go and take out the rubbish and stop worrying. You're still a long way off from choosing a profession."

I remained standing there in the middle of the kitchen, holding the smelly rubbish bag that held the remains of the fish we'd had for lunch and bits and pieces from mum's sewing, and said that, for the time being, I was best at throwing out the rubbish. How come I'd moved from doing it only on Saturdays, to doing it every day, I asked. I'd developed a talent for throwing out the rubbish. I knew how to pick the right time when it was quiet in the hallway and loud on the other side of the doors and walls. I knew I had to hold the rubbish bag away from me so that I wouldn't get dirty. The worst moment was when I had to open the wheelie bin in the courtyard. That was when all the imaginable and unimaginable smells that people left behind came flying out. They say on TV that one day people will be suffocated by the amount of rubbish they've piled up. There's an accumulation of so many unnecessary things. While some people are overeating, others are starving. Starvation leads to death, but so can overeating. The world is sinking into an im-ba-lance. I don't know about the world, but I'm constantly teetering, losing my balance, when I find myself next to the rubbish bin and wheelie. Because I try to keep the air out of my lungs by not breathing for a bit.

Nobody in our building has thrown out as much rubbish as I have, especially if I count the professor. In other families they take turns throwing out the rubbish. I know because I can see them through the window. Sometimes I even hear them arguing in their flats, over who took the rubbish out the last time and whose turn it was now. In our house it's always my turn, I'm the only one who does it all the time. Maybe I'll become a rubbish collector. I just wanted to know what she thought about the idea and so in the end I asked her.

"That's nonsense! Of course you're not going to be a dustman. Where did you get such an idea? You're just helping me with ordinary household chores, that's all. I can't do everything myself, now can I?! And anyway, why should I? The fact that you've got certain difficulties doesn't mean you have to be spared doing chores."

"I could do the dusting, like you. Or make pies. I'm better at exercising my hands than my feet.

She sighed.

"I once told you, remember, when Natalia invited you to her birthday party and you didn't go, that you have to practice your social skills. The rubbish has nothing to do with your feet, it has to do with your social skills. Which means that as soon as you walk out this door, with your schoolbag on your back or rubbish bag in your hand, or whatever, you'll run into somebody, somebody will say *good morning* or *good afternoon*, somebody will ask you something. It's important for you to be in contact with people, for you to communicate. I see no chance for your progress if you stay at home and do the dusting with me."

"I can progress by throwing out the rubbish?"

"If I didn't know you so well, and didn't know how you like to tease, I'd think you were doing this deliberately! C'mon, take the rubbish bag and get a move on, already. Enough talk."

"But…what's wrong with dustmen? Tonko is always throwing stones at their trucks."

"Nothing's wrong with them. They earn their money by honest work, like anybody else. Tonko's upbringing smells more than the rubbish in the rubbish truck. Everybody knows that. You're too impressed by that boy, you know! Every so often I hear you say: Tonko this, Tonko that…"

"He's going to be a writer. And a cartoonist."

"We have yet to see what he'll be. He's got a lot of writing and drawing to do before that. In any case, a writer should be a cultured person and sensitive to other people's stories and interests. He's certainly none of that right now."

"Can I at least go downstairs in my slippers?"

"No. You know you can't and stop asking me because I'm not going to change my mind. Stop philosophizing and get going already. Today you have permission to go out as far as the park. I'm cleaning the flat and I don't want you under my feet. Alright?"

I was having trouble with my shoes and laces and the word "patience" was not part of her vocabulary today. She looked at her watch, sighed, bent down, took two seconds to tie them and said:

"Come on, come on, I don't have time to wait for you. The next time you'll have to do it yourself. Get going, already..."

And so, I went.

I stepped into the lift and pressed the button that said 1. It's not that I made a mistake. I knew the difference between G. and the number 1. No, I did it deliberately. Because I missed Professor Antun. I missed him even though I didn't like taking his rubbish out. I liked him for a well-known reason. As soon as the lift creaked to a stop, I opened the door and looked at his front door. The mat wasn't there anymore. Nor the bag of rubbish. Nor the shoebox. Nothing was there, not even his name-plate. One day some people came and carried everything out of his flat. A lot of the junk (that's what mum called his things) wound up in or in front of the wheelie. They especially had trouble with the piano. Naturally, the instrument didn't go onto the rubbish heap, although I'd hoped it would. I thought that if nobody needed it maybe mum would let us have it. Unfortunately, that didn't happen. They lifted it onto the truck and drove if off somewhere.

As for the lift, I'd been doing that ever since he died. I'd press the button for the first floor, look at his door as if to say hello or something, and then I'd press G. This time, as soon as the lift door closed, somebody called it to go up.

A lady for whom mum does dress alterations got in on the eighth floor. I couldn't remember her name, but she knew mine right away:

"Emil, you're here! Did you mistake the floors?"

I shook my head.

"You didn't? So, you just like riding in the lift?"

I shook my head again, because I didn't like it at all.

"Aha, let me guess again, you don't know your letters and numbers well yet, is that it?"

I nodded, because that was true, at least regarding numbers.

"When you go to throw out the rubbish, now watch, you have press here, G for Ground Floor! Remember G! G!

"I know, I'm not stupid…," I said, after which she stopped smiling and asking me questions. I had none for her. Although maybe I should have one or two, to practice my social skills. But I couldn't think of any, except to ask when she'd come back for mum to widen her dress again because you could see that this one was too tight. You always have to leave an extra two or three centimetres to let the body breathe. Mum says that we don't breathe just through our mouth and nose, but through our skin as well. That's why it's not good if things are tight. Plus, if the fabric is synthetic, then that's a double disaster. It may be the fashion but it's not healthy, mum says. But I didn't feel like discussing health with the lady from the eighth floor. Because then she might ask me if I was healthy. Naturally, I'm healthy, but I just can't run. And that doesn't have anything to do with health anyway. And maybe she wouldn't understand what I was talking about. Or I wouldn't know how to explain it properly. Maybe she didn't care about health the way I did. Maybe that would lead to a misunderstanding.

We rode down in silence. We parted with her saying:

"Have a nice day, Emil, and say hello to your mum."

It can't be a nice day if you have to start it by taking out the rubbish. Full stop! Plus, I felt bad because she was sure to have decided that I was stupid. Because of the lift. And the G button.

On the ground floor I climbed onto the wooden chair and peered into the letterboxes. Even though I'd promised mum not to do it anymore, I simply couldn't get out of the habit. All the letterboxes were more or less empty, except for Professor Antun's; he was still getting bills as if he owed somebody something here on earth. I'm not sure what happens when you die leaving behind a debt. How do you repay it? Who would repay my debt to Instantly? How many tailored suits would it take to satisfy him?

As soon as I went out, I saw a box on the little wall by the wheelie.

When I went over to it, I saw that it wasn't just any box. It was a shoebox! A shoebox!

Mum says I have two ob-sessions. Ob-session number 1 is snow. Ob-session number 2 is shoeboxes! As for this last one I can say one thing: there are no special boxes for special shoes. None. And let me say right off, I wouldn't collect them even if they existed. No way! I know they'd be as ugly as the shoes themselves. I can just imagine a box that would say, not Adidas or Nike, but *Uncle Mario*! Disaster! On the other hand, something that doesn't get you anywhere, how can that be nice? Something that doesn't make you grow. Or your muscles or body grow. Something that does nothing. Zero. O.

Eager to grab the box, I decided to quickly get rid of the rubbish. Quickly meant choosing a faster-than-usual way to throw out the rubbish. The wheelie was already open and overflowing, so I simply swung the bag into the air and...missed!

That same moment the bag split open and the smelly fish bones, along with everything else, came flying out.

Well, that was enough to drive you mad! If I didn't sit down and cry then, I never would! What to do? Gather it all up or not? I opted to gather it up, however long it took and however disgusting it was, because the rubbish was mine, and it's not good to pollute the environment, plus Mr. Franjo might turn up. I had bad luck with him. He always ran into me at the worst possible moment. He might start listing my offences again. Broken windows! Destroyed social property! Spilt rubbish bags! And I didn't want him to call me a pest again!

I'd never done anything so disgusting before. It was as if I was practicing for the job I'd be doing in the future. My hands got all filthy. But in the end, I managed to pick everything up and throw it into the wheelie. I had no choice but to wipe my hands on my trousers and jacket. I looked up at the balconies. No sight of *It's Good to Do Good.* In fact, no sight of anybody. It was just me and the rubbish.

The colour and picture on the box sitting on the wall kept drawing my attention. Now that my trousers were greasy, but my hands dry and only a bit sticky from the oil of the fish bones, I had no reason to wait. Lifting it off the wall, I was surprised by how heavy the shoebox was. I'd thought it would be empty and light.

But it was when I opened it that I was left speechless...

Inside were a not exactly new or clean pair of children's trainers, with stick-on straps!! I think that in my case that's what you'd call a double jackpot! The box plus the trainers!

I was lucky because they were two sizes too big for me. Luckily, they weren't two sizes too small! Because then I would have simply sat down and cried.

Nobody could see me behind the two big green over-flowing wheelie bins and the little stone wall. The smell was worse than where I'd been waiting for the client who never showed up. There was rubbish everywhere, making it a safe place for not running into anyone. Everybody avoided spending even a second more than they had to in that place.

When I took out the trainers, I could see that whoever had worn them had had no problem running or walking. The back and front were scuffed, the soles were worn out and the straps loose. The top of the right trainer had a hole! I ran my hand over them, imagining them on my feet, walking, kicking a ball, climbing up, climbing down, running… This was the perfect opportunity to stop imagining and to put them on.

I sat down on the ground and started taking off my special shoes. It took forever. There seemed to be no end to…the torture.

But…oh boy when I finally put the trainers on!!! And quickly stuck on that loose strap! And stood up! And walked! It was something indescribable…Well, I suppose it could be described as: walking on a cloud. Or as my heart growing wings.

They flapped a little and my toe stuck out through the hole a little when I walked, and I think something stuck to the back of my trousers when I sat down on the ground, but…who cared! I was so happy I sang to myself: *Tralala-la…la!*

I still wasn't sure what I would do with them. I put my special shoes in the box and left it on the wall. I decided I'd come back for them once I'd finished breaking in the trainers. But first I'd pop over to the park, sit on the bench, then come back to the rubbish bin, take my special shoes and…ask mum if I could keep the trainers since they didn't belong to anybody? Or maybe I wouldn't tell her anything - I'd considered that as well. I could put them at the back of the wardrobe with the other boxes and wear them when the opportunity arose. I mean, all sorts of ideas occurred to me. All sorts!

I climbed back up onto the wall again, peered out over the mound of rubbish in the wheelie bin, took a few soft, soundless steps, keeping my eye on them, when, like a bolt out of the blue, I heard a voice:

"Emil? Are you Emil Vidić? I hope I'm not mistaken…"

I froze when I recognized the voice of Miss Dunja, the social worker who liked sticking her nose into other people's business and asking questions of strangers. Because that was the kind of work she did, according to *It's Good to Do Good.*

I nodded. Because how could I lie that I wasn't who I was? Maybe in my place Tonko would have said it wasn't him. Maybe he would have said: that's not me, you made a mistake. Maybe he'd even use some bad language. Or maybe he'd run as far away as he could, his laughter trailing behind him in the air. Because he always found a reason to laugh. Unlike me. Right now, I couldn't do anything that he could. Not anything. Zero. O.

"Alright then, I was just coming to see you, to see what you're up to, but I didn't expect to find you here. How on earth did you get in and out of that smelly wheelie bin? My goodness, you're filthy and…"

I didn't say anything. She didn't understand that I'd just found the one thing I wanted more than anything else in the world. She didn't have a problem with her trainers so she couldn't understand. I thought to myself: who knows if the social worker has a problem of her own? If she does, then who was sticking their nose into *her* business? And what difference did it make if I got a bit dirty? What did she care? She wouldn't be washing my trousers and jacket, mum would. Well, the washing machine would.

"Come here, come, come, why are you frozen to the spot, come closer so I can get a good look at you...What on earth is that on your feet?

"Trainers."

"So I see! But isn't it time to get a new pair? Your mum doesn't walk around in rags, so I see no reason why she should dress you like this. You're not that poor. It's not right for you to rummage through the rubbish and walk around in torn shoes."

"Trainers."

"Whatever, as long as you are clean and neat. Did your mum see how you were dressed when you went out today?"

"Naturally," I said, immediately taking mum's side. I said that she always laid out my clothes and sometimes helped me with them. Sometimes she let me dress myself, for the exercise. Today she helped me because my fingers cramped.

"Interesting...And where is your mum now? Is she at home?"

I said she was.

"Is she alone?"

"Aha."

"Fine. Then you and I will now go upstairs together. We'll have a little chat. Come..."

"I have to go...to the park."

"The park? On your own? Looking like that? Take a look at yourself!"

"!!!"

OK, maybe they weren't top-notch trainers, but still, they were my first pair. I didn't feel like going upstairs with her, full stop! She'd ruined everything. So it was that kind of morning after all, a BAD morning! And no *good morning* could change that. It had gone bad just when I thought that finding the box would make it a good morning. We set off together and I remembered the story that Miss Dunja could separate people, if she decided that was for the better, though I didn't know for whom it would be for the better! I didn't want to be separated from mum, no way. Let that be known! No way! And I'd tell her so if she asked me. For the moment, though, she wasn't asking me anything. That's to say, she was asking, but without using the word *separation*. I didn't know how whales resolved these things if somebody came to separate them.

We didn't talk on the way up, that's to say she asked questions: about mum, about me, about school, but I didn't have any more to say than I'd said already. I waited carefully for the word *separation,* I didn't want to miss it, so I could tell her that it was out of the question, but it didn't arise. I didn't speak, I was still thinking about the separated whales in the sea. I didn't want to tell her what I was thinking. Because she would have certainly been surprised and said: "How's that relevant, that's not what we're discussing." Then I would start explaining that it was relevant, because it was similar, and then maybe everything would end badly. For me.

When we arrived at our front door, I went to ring the doorbell, but Miss Dunja stopped me:

"Wait! Why ring the bell when you've got the key hanging around your neck? Why did your mum give you the key anyway?"

"In case…she by chance…wasn't…at home."

"By chance? That's what she also said that time when you were at home alone, sick. That time she said she'd just popped out to the pharmacy for a second. Is that where she went or did she go to work?"

I was just about to explain what had happened, but at the last minute I changed my mind. Because, as usual, everything I said could sound confused. It would be the same with my whale story. So I simply shrugged my shoulders and reached out to press the bell again

"I told you to try the key, not the bell. Did you hear what I said?"

"But…mum…is inside."

"I believe you. Let's surprise her."

Why? Who likes unpleasant surprises? I was sure that mum wouldn't jump with joy at the sight of her. I certainly hadn't. She'd appeared like a bolt out of the blue. And nobody likes bolts. When there's a blue sky, you expect only the sun and wind, but this was - *wham*!

My hands were sweaty and I couldn't fit the key into the lock on the first go. I never do. I can barely manage to do it when I'm by myself, let alone if somebody is watching me. Then she said: "Do you want me to try?" I wouldn't let her. I hoped that mum might hear me fiddling with the lock and would come and open the door herself. But she didn't. It was hard but finally I unlocked the door.

As soon as we walked in, I wanted to somehow signal that we were there. That there were two of us. Miss Dunja and me. But I got tongue-tied. And even worse, so did Miss Dunja. She didn't even say "Good morning". Or: "Knock-knock, anybody home?" Nothing. Not a word.

And then we heard, not mum hoovering, but voices in the kitchen. One was mum's and the other was a man's. I recognized it immediately. The two of us stood in the hallway, listening. That's called eavesdropping. Now it was more than obvious that Miss Dunja was sticking her nose into other people's busines. I wasn't sticking my nose into anything because it was my mum and our flat. So I just listened, but she eavesdropped. The conversation in the kitchen went something like this:

"Think it over some more."

"There's nothing to think over. I don't intend to have any more children. Not with anybody. It's got nothing to do with you. Anyway, what are we talking about? What's love got to do with it?"

"Of course it's got something to do with it. At least as far as I'm concerned. As for children…"

"I'm telling you again that wanting children is your problem, not mine."

"I'd say that right now you and I have a joint problem, since you've decided to tell me about it, though I don't see it as a problem, I see it as an opportunity. Anyway, how often do I have to tell you that I've started divorce proceedings. And, in the final analysis, why shouldn't your son finally have a dad?"

"Don't worry about Emil's dad! The fact that you don't know who he is doesn't mean he doesn't exist."

"And what role does this invisible man currently have in his life?"

"That's no concern of yours."

"Maybe. But it is to him. Except he's unable to use his tongue and ask for answers. I'm afraid that in that respect, and with such a mother, he is still groping in the darkness of ignorance..."

"You know what I think? I think it's not nice to sow your seed all over the place. Keeping children within the walls of a house is a skill. And you've already got a house. And children. And a wife. Do you think they'd be happy to learn that they'd be getting someone like Emil for a brother? There are easy and difficult kinds of love in life, and you yourself know which category Emil belongs to. Would they be able to deal with that? Would you?"

"Speaking of categories, ha!, you don't fall into the easy category either. I wouldn't try if I didn't think I could do it. Do you know that I boxed when I was young and I had challengers from heavier categories than yours. So there."

"No, really, no joking, do you think you could love him the way you say you love me? I wouldn't ask for anything less."

"That's really not fair, Marina. I didn't say that you'd have to love my children straight off the bat. These things come gradually. They can't be forced. You chose a bad example. But I'd try, I'd make an effort to..."

"And then you'd give up when you didn't succeed..."

"Look, if you don't start something, there's nothing to give up on. You've given up before you even started.

On yourself. On others. I'm not afraid of new beginnings. I'm not stuck in a rut, like you, looking back at the past. For you, the present boils down to counting other people's wrong moves. Your understanding of cowardice is based on your own bad experience. You don't really want me to succeed with you in this. Because I'm not the issue, you are. Because what if you don't succeed? What if what you have with me becomes yet another one of your failures? You're looking for fucking poor reasons to justify your feeble excuses, Marina."

"Honestly, Igor, have you ever really tried to be in my shoes, in my skin, other than having blackmailed your way into my knickers?"

"Oho! And what exactly do you know about my shoes? Nothing. Except that you didn't think twice about acquainting yourself with my… boxer shorts!"

"Don't make me remind you how that… acquaintanceship came about! You want me to talk about the blackmail?"

"I'd rather go back to the shoes. You see, I never offered them to you, though I could have. Let's say I offered you the best of myself: love and sex. Because to walk in my shoes is heavy shit. Maybe even more so than to walk in yours. Maybe it's better you don't know. So don't wave that in front of my nose because you can't see beyond your own nose. But if you'd ever really wanted to know what it's like to be in my shoes, I wouldn't have stopped you. So, as far as … our underwear is concerned, I am telling you and maintain that we started off with the better part of ourselves. We left our shoes under the bed, and it's better that way…I never claimed to be a saint. Maybe my methods to have you at any cost weren't up to the mark, but you're not damned innocent either, so don't talk to me about how decent you are and how you were seduced. I've always been clear about my feelings for you, but you've consistently sent mixed signals. A bit hot, then a bit cold. Love and sex are enough for any beginning. Every step after that is a good beginning."

"I don't believe it's good to build a beginning on the ruins of somebody's else's end."

"You didn't cause anything on my side that hadn't already collapsed of itself. You know everything, you're just pretending to forget because right now it suits you that way. You just don't want to hear me say that I love you. As for the man you've been seeing recently, yes, yes, don't deny it, don't be surprised, his name is Nikola, I know everything, I've got my own sources, does he even know about you and me and what's going on between us?"

"Let me be clear, I'm not seeing anybody! He teaches at Emil's school. He's a friend, a support, nothing more."

"A support, a friend, nothing more. Interesting. Why, then, doesn't the support support you anymore? Why don't you see the support anymore? Don't make lunch for the support anymore? Did things break down with him the way it did with us? Or are you going to say that nothing broke down between us because there was nothing there to start with. And your condition has to do with the Holy Spirit? Hallelujah, Marina!"

"Igor, I don't want to talk anymore. My friendship with that man is my private affair, so I'm asking you nicely..."

"I repeat, does your support know what physical condition you're currently in?"

"Igor, we said what we had to say, so if you're thinking of continuing to blackmail me..."

"We haven't said everything and stop using the word blackmail. Somebody might think I'm exerting force on you. Force is how you want to get rid of me. Politely and with kid gloves. Lady-like! I want you to get some rest. Take the day off and think everything over..."

"Listen, I've got a lot of work and Emil is about to come back any minute, so please just go now..."

At that moment, Miss Dunja, still in the hallway, decided to cough. I shifted from one foot to the other. We heard the two of them in the kitchen suddenly fall silent, and then mum said:

"Who's there? Emil, is that you?"

She opened the kitchen door and looked at us in astonishment. As if we were a couple of ghosts whose eyes glowed in the dark.

"Now this is what I call a surprise! Miss Dunja! Where did you come from? How did you get into the flat?"

"Why, with Emil's key, how else? Forgive me for bothering you and interrupting your conversation. I decided to drop by today..."

Igor stood up without a word, took his rustling jacket and, without saying goodbye, walked out of the flat. Then mum said:

"Emil? Take a look at yourself. What's that on your feet?"

"That's what I asked him, Marina."

"Where are your shoes? Where did you leave your shoes, Emil, do you hear what I'm asking you?"

"I hear."

"??" (mum's raised eyebrows like two question marks)

"By the wheelie bin."

"By the wheelie bin? But why? What are they doing there? Go downstairs and bring them back. This minute!

The two of us will wait for you. Would you like a cup of coffee, Miss Dunja?" mum said, her voice softer, a stampede thundering in her chest.

I took the lift down and went outside. The wheelie was still full of rubbish, but the shoebox was nowhere in sight. Nowhere!

The "Noises" Bakery

SOMEBODY IN the schoolyard said that the Blessed Mother had appeared in the school corridor. Everybody ran to see if it was true. Tonko ran off, swearing at the bearer of the news:

"You better not be bullshitting! I'll fuck your mother if you're lying!"

Naturally, that was something everybody wanted to see. The dirty words part. Because the news about the Blessed Mother didn't sound true, as we would discover when we got to the school corridor. Alright, not everybody ran there. We know who was trailing behind. I was wearing my old special shoes, because the new ones hadn't yet been made. Plus, mum said that I had better start thinking about who would be holding down my foot for an impression at Uncle Mario's this time. Because it wasn't going to be her!

"Who then?" I asked, worried.

"I don't care! You dare to ask me that after everything that's happened?", she said, angrily ending the conversation so that I didn't ask any more questions.

We didn't find my new special shoes although later we spent a long time looking for them around the rubbish bins and peering into the wheelie. Somebody had stolen them along with the shoe box and I couldn't figure out who would think of doing such a silly thing! Didn't they know that the shoes wouldn't take them far? And that they'd attract *those looks*. We threw the trainers with the hole into the wheelie bin, but only because mum firmly promised this time to buy me new ones.

"With my first salary," she said, "although you don't deserve them considering that incident with the rubbish. You almost ruined everything with Miss Dunja. She couldn't have seen you in a worse situaiton and to tell you the truth, neither could I. And you brought her into the flat without warning! I'd spent all that time preparing you for her and for the possibility of such a situation, only for you to quietly bring her into the flat like a common-or-garden spy. Not to mention the trainers by the rubbish bins. It took superhuman effort on my part to persuade the woman how much you wanted to have them like all the other children. Then she started talking about her own children's mishaps. And that's where it somehow ended. I say *somehow,* because you made it possible for her to eavesdrop in the hallway and to pry into things that she didn't need to know. So, because I don't want you to get any more silly ideas, be they physical or otherwise, you'll get the trainers. I promise! But you won't be wearing the key around your neck anymore. Because you either lose it or unlock the door for the wrong people!"

But to get back to the Blessed Mother.

You could see her glowing from far away, so nothing came of those dirty words that Tonko had maybe been hoping for at the beginning. She was standing on an elevation, holding a crown in her hand. Behind her was a plastic rock, and in front a vase with artificial flowers.

The excitement over this unusual event did not last long. Because nobody wanted to follow the religious teacher's suggestion that we kneel and pray. Except for the pupils who wanted to get a better grade in religious studies. It wasn't me who said that, it was somebody in the crowd who was heard to say that this was an ideal opportunity to get a better grade without much effort. As for the pupils who didn't care about their grades, they didn't feel like kneeling and praying because the first class of the day was religious studies anyway. After most of the children left, I went up to the Blessed Mother myself. Down by the bench, the religion teacher was praying alongside two girls from my class. She beckoned me closer and said I could join them. She said that the Blessed Mother didn't mind if you attended religious studies for real or just sat there. She loved all people equally and made no difference between them. When I said the word *apparition,* she corrected me:

"Emil, she did not appear, the school's director, Mr. Buškulić, had the sculpture brought here. It was made by a sculptor friend of his, who, in addition to being a great artist is also a great believer. Come, we're all now going to pray together for both of them, and for Our Lady to bless everyone, and for you to attend religious studies for real next year."

We'd just started saying "Our Father, Who art in heaven," (they out loud and me to myself) when a woman appeared behind us. Maybe it was somebody's mother, I don't know exactly.

"Am I lost? Where am I? In a church or in a school? What kind of circus is this?"

"Madam, watch your words!" retorted the religion teacher, rising to her feet from the bench.

"Who installed – this? It didn't appear by itself, I suppose?"

"First of all, it's not a *this,* it's a sculpture of the Blessed Mother. Children, go to your classroom now," she said, hurrying us off. "And you, Madam, let's hear what's actually bothering you. The sculpture of Our Lady is standing in front of my classroom. Just as there is a picture of Nikola Tesla hanging in front of the physics room. What's the problem?"

"Certainly not Nikola Tesla. If he were alive, even he wouldn't manage to light up the darkness that reigns in some minds today. Faith is a private matter, and its place is either in the home or in church. We are a state school, not a private school. And because of that I am going to report you and Mr. Buškulić to the Ministry. But before that I'm going to bring over some journalists, they'll feed on your blood..."

The religion teacher finally pushed us into the classroom and closed the door. She continued with the argument from the corridor even though it was time for our lesson. And when she finished, the class naturally moved on to praying for, as she said, a successful conclusion to the problem of the sculpture of Our Lady.

Our next class was with our regular teacher. We immediately started rehearsing for the play. We pushed the desks up against the wall and took the costumes mum had made out of the wardrobe. There were costumes for all sorts of things: a snowflake, a ball, a star, gifts. OK, I figured that not everybody would like them. There weren't that many. And I knew that not everybody could take part in the play. Maybe the best pupils. But I figured that if even Tonko could get a role despite all the 2s he had in the grade book, then surely I would be given something as well. I was the only one left sitting on the school bench, wringing my hands under my desk. Something I otherwise do only in maths class or when the teacher starts asking me questions.

At one point, the teacher sat on my desk. Just like the last time. From there she observed the scene in front of her. Her stomach was again too close to my ear. And…there was no mistake about it. The sound was still there: soft, rustling, flaky, quiet, flickering.

"Miss…"

She didn't hear me at first, she was busy correcting the children who were singing, reciting, acting.

"Miss…" I said a bit louder.

"What is it, Emil?"

"Will I…appear too?"

She thought for a minute before saying:

"You will. Be patient. There's time. Your part is simple. You won't have to say anything, you'll be a gift under the Christmas tree."

"I'd like to be…a snowflake. I like…snowflakes."

"I know. But these snowflakes talk and move around the stage."

"That's what…real ones do…too."

"I'm sorry? What do they do?"

"They talk and move."

I think the phrase is: she was left speechless!

"I know…how to move," I went on.

"Emil, I've already handed out the parts to the other children. If you'd been more cooperative this term, you could have been whatever you wanted. Come. I'll dress you in your costume so you can rehearse the scene under the tree."

And here we hit a snag. I wanted to put it on by myself. She wanted to help. We couldn't do it without her touching my head and hair. Then she said: "Never mind, you sit under the tree and pretend to be the gift without your costume on."

I was immediately sorry I'd asked her anything. It would have been better if I had stayed sitting on the school bench, looking out the window. Who'd want me as a present under the tree? No-one except for mum. But I would have been a perfect rustling snowflake. If only she had let me show her.

At the end of the class, while I waited for the others to leave the classroom one by one, the teacher called me over.

"Emil, come here. Can I ask you something?"

I nodded my head. I thought that maybe she was going to say something about the part she'd given me. When…

"You know, if I'd heard it from anybody else, I wouldn't have believed it, but it was Professor Nikola. He says, um, that you can hear…actually that you heard two hearts beating inside me."

I didn't say anything, I just waited for her question. That's what she said, "I'll ask you something."

She continued, because I kept my mouth shut.

"So, if he isn't lying, are you?"

"I never…lie."

"Really? Never ever? Then how do you know about it?"

"I heard it."

"From whom?"

"From myself."

"I think you heard it too, but from somebody in the street or in school. Admit it."

I shook my head and looked down.

"Alright, I'm not going to insist because I don't want you to burst into tears, and I don't need any more problems with either you or your mother, but you'll be hard put to convince me that it's something you can hear, just like that. There's another thing that interests me. Do you know where that other heart inside me came from?"

Now that's what I call a question! I quickly shook my head and looked at her. I hadn't a clue. It had a nice sound but that's all I could say about it.

"I'm going to have a baby. The second heart is the baby's."

Ooooh…! My jaw dropped. So that's what it was! And mum was going to have a baby too!? And I was going to have a brother or sister? What a surprise!

"But…how did the baby get…inside?" I wanted to know, pointing at her tummy.

"Now that's a question for your mother. Let her explain it to you."

The school playground was empty when I left, but my head was full of questions. I hadn't taken more than a few steps along the surrounding concrete wall when I noticed Instantly on the other side of the street. He beckoned me over, just the way the teacher had done a little while ago. I knew why he was there and why he needed me. It made my legs turn to wood. I felt as if I was walking for a long, long time. But all I had to do was cross the road.

He opened the back door of the Audi. Which meant: get in and don't ask any questions. That's how we always started driving. In silence. With the smell of sweets. With him adjusting the rear-view mirror. Checking the road. With me waiting for him to speak first. He took off his sunglasses. And he was a sight to see. He had two big purple blotches under his eyes. This time I pretended not to see them. I didn't want him to say "mind your own business", like the last time. So, minding my own business, I looked away and gazed out of the window. The roads and traffic lights flew by, making the city look unreal.

"I hope that thing is in a safe place. Is it?" he suddenly asked. "Great. That female from last time…just to be clear, the bitch wanted to set me up! But I smelled the cops on time. She couldn't figure you out. So, it's in a safe place, you say?" He looked at me in the rear-view mirror and I nodded again that it was, although it wasn't.

I think that was the first time it dawned on me that I had no choice but to lie. Even though I had just told the teacher that I never lie. Even though I always say the same thing, if somebody asks me. Now here I was lying, without a blink of an eye. I realized that if I stuck to the truth, I'd be in trouble this time. I remembered that he had told me more than once: "Cut the crap, sometimes you gotta lie!" Well, what else was I doing except nodding my head at the exact moment when I'd otherwise be shaking it. The only thing that worried me was that he would somehow hear the lie or that it would show on me. But either I was a good liar or he'd decided to believe me, one friend to another. The truth is I had no idea where the packet in the popcorn had ended up. Probably in the rubbish heap. Maybe it was being recycled right now. I saw on TV that that's what they do with some rubbish. Which, despite the good side of re-cycling, was still bad news for Instantly.

"OK. Keep it a little while longer because it's not safe with me. I'm curious: where did you hide it this time? We've ditched the piggybank, I suppose?"

"It's in…the popcorn."

"Since then? No shit! And your mother? She hasn't cottoned on?"

I shook my head.

"When I was your age, my old lady used to stick her trunk of a nose into every piece of shit I brought home. Truth is I got into all sorts of trouble and once bitten; the poor old thing was twice shy..."

I didn't get the part about the trunk or the "twice shy" bit. I didn't say anything though, hoping that we'd somehow move on from the popcorn and packet. Because I hadn't figured out how to keep on lying about it.

"I know your mother is at home now, so we won't go there now to get it. We'll leave it for another time."

He surprised me! How did he know about mum? But that's not what I asked him, what I asked was:

"With the piece of wire?"

"What wire?"

He thought for a second, and then quickly remembered.

"Aha...Of course, with the piece of wire. Since you're clumsy and lose your keys. When I was little..."

Now he was into stories about when he was little...

"...I remember, my old man used to beat me like a donkey. He'd take off his belt and use the end with the metal buckle, so it would hurt more. Once he went at me with his hands and feet because I'd lost the key to the flat and I wound up in hospital. My old lady told everybody that I'd fallen off the scaffolding. Nobody believed her, but she stuck to her story, and then so did I. When we came home, with me all bruised and patched up, he went for her because he hadn't had his dinner, he was hungry, waiting for her to bring me back from the hospital. But I never cried. And my mother didn't either. Only pussies cry. You ever cry?"

I quickly shook my head, though I knew that if I continued like this I'd be like St. Peter. He lied about Jesus in the Garden of Gethsemane. Afterwards he regretted it and cried. He hid his face in shame and cried. I was sure that Instantly would use that dirty word for him too if he knew what had happened to Jesus. Judas would have fared even worse. Because nobody likes snitches. As Instantly once explained it, a snitch is …

"In those days we didn't have…fucking hell, what do you call those phones: blue, red, purple, brave, sad…I don't know, it doesn't matter, because in those days you could either be fucked by your problems or get out of the house and look for a place under the sun."

We drove in silence again, each caught up in our own thoughts, except that he said, more to himself than to me:

"Fuck it. You've reminded me of all the crap I had with my old man…"

"I don't have…a dad."

"You're better off that way! I'm not gonna be anybody's dad either. See? See how us two can have a nice conversation when we want? Especially when we start with our fucked-up families. We'd have done better sticking a finger into a pile of shit and stirring it. It wouldn't have left such a bad smell…"

"Why don't you want to be…a dad?"

"Because I'll croak before then. Somebody'll bump me off and…end of story. Hey! I'm kidding! Don't look at me with those eyes. Listen, it's better for a degenerate family line like mine to die out with me. Maybe I'd beat up my son the way my old man beat me up. Who knows? It can get into your blood. Like a kind of family bacteria. One Instantly in the world is enough. Who needs two, three…"

His mobile rang. Somebody at the other end kept talking while Instantly just listened, swallowing his saliva, one of his eyelids twitching though he tried to calm it with his finger.

"No worries, bro," he said when he finally managed to get a word in. "It's all here. It's here, I tell you! You just get a new pack of tiles ready. The Italian ones. I want two square meters with glazing. They gotta be first class. Where did you say? OK! How many? It's a deal. At the 'Romeo' café in half an hour."

"We're going for a minute to pick something up," he said, explaining that I would take some of what he was collecting. I would hide it in some brilliant, crazy place until he felt that the danger, at least as far as he was concerned, had passed. He didn't believe anybody anymore. It was a disgrace what he'd been reduced to. To children. The disabled. He must be disabled himself. In the head.

"Agreed?"

Aha, I said to myself, nodding. Since nobody was asking for my help. Since nobody believed me. Not Mr. Franjo. Not the teacher. Not Professor Nikola. The only problem was that I didn't know what to do with the tiles and how to hide them. They were big and heavy. How was I going to carry them?

When we arrived, he told me to lie down and hide under the seat, I was so small nobody would see me.

"Don't raise your head, we don't want any crap about who you are and what the fuck you're doing in my car! This is a fucked-up world, in case you didn't know. I'm a nobody compared to these guys. And they're nobodies compared to some other guys, except, as you'll find out one day, they all like to strut their stuff in front of smaller fry. They like pretending they're bigshots. Anyway, I can't keep inventing cousins and brothers. They're not that stupid. That's to say, they are but for this sort of stuff they're masters."

Before curling up on the floor of the car, I'd noticed that there was no café in sight. And there was nothing called "Romeo". There was a lot of mud, a lonely bakery and lots of unfinished houses. There was the smell of freshly baked bread. The bakery was called "Noises", as in a racket, a din, which couldn't be heard anywhere, other than in his chest. Instantly switched from his Audi to another car, an Alfa Romeo. That was the only Romeo around.

I could hear them through the open window, arguing over the price of the tiles.

"What fucking interest?" Instantly shouted. "I don't have it! That's not what we fucking agreed!"

Then the other man said that next time he'd give the better product to somebody more reliable and leave the scrap for him. And then what would he do? Who was going to buy stuff like that from him? And those plums under his eyes would be nothing compared to what he could do to him. His own mother wouldn't recognize him!

"Don't you mention my dead old lady! I'll bring you the rest tomorrow. You have my word. I give you my word!" Instantly shouted.

"Your word is worth less than a whore's fart! You understand me? You know how many characters like you I've already iced for lying? Well, you'll be joining a slew of them in twenty-four hours if I don't see that dosh!"

Instantly got back into the car and said:

"Don't you dare get up until I give you a sign. And don't breathe. You don't exist, you understand? That fucking gang of robbers and their fucking 'interest'..."

Snow

THE DAY of the school play finally arrived. After lunch, mum wanted to know if I had a part. I nodded yes, but I didn't tell her not to expect too much of the stupid non-speaking gift. "Alright, then don't tell me anything, let it be a surprise," she said. That didn't make me particularly happy. The only things that did were the overcast sky, grey clouds and the good weather forecast. She went to the bathroom to get ready for work, and I followed her. If I wasn't doing my homework or watching a movie, I'd follow her from room to room, which sometimes got on her nerves because she'd tell me not to be at her heels like a dog. She needed a break too sometimes. It would be nice if she could at least go to the toilet and do her business there without me knocking at the door, asking when she was coming out.

"It's going to snow," I said, although I meant to say something else, not that, but I didn't know how to begin. "Look at the sky. It's going to snow for sure this time…" I continued, still on the other subject.

"We're not going to stare at the sky and fantasize, Emil, because we don't have the time. Auntie Zrinka is going to lend us her car so we won't have to walk in the cold tonight. And later, if we feel like it, we can drop by her place. I haven't been behind the wheel in donkey's years. I just hope the road will stay dry. And you stop obsessing about the snow!"

"Mum…"

"Yes?"

"Professor Nikola said to tell you..." was what I had to say to her.

"Enough already! How many times must I tell you not to mention him anymore? How many times? Do you understand the meaning of the words NEVER AGAIN!" she said, turning to face me, holding a brush tangled with hair. It was the same when I'd tried these past few days to give her his message - she refused to listen. She'd just say, "Enough, stop, I don't want to hear it!" Even though the message was simple and not complicated at all. It said she should call him on his mobile or land line. That's all. I realized that after that lunch the two of them had got into a tangle, like the hair in mum's brush, but who knew why or how. If mum was a good person, and Professor Nikola was a good person, then what was the tangle about? That's what I asked myself.

"But why?"

"Because!"

"But how come?"

"And don't mention the teacher either!" she added, though I hadn't mentioned her. "Sending me enigmatic messages through you. *Ask your mum how babies enter the tummy,*" she said, distorting her voice to imitate her. "The next time your teacher sends a message for me, I suggest you ask *him*. Let him tell you how the baby entered her tummy."

"Why him? It's her tummy, not his..."

"And speaking of babies..." she interrupted me, "I've told you that I'm not having one. Did you put your ear on my tummy the other day? You did. Was there anything to hear? No there wasn't! Full stop! End of story!"

"I'd like a brother or a sister."

"I'd like lots of things in life, but I don't have them. Not a decent job, not a flat. I work myself to the bone all day, I don't have a single friend left. Like in the book *Palle Alone in the World.* That's what I've become…alone."

"I don't have any either."

"You and I aren't the same. I had friends; you have to try and make some, and I mean try. You can't expect them to fall out of the sky just like that, because friends don't fall…like snowflakes. And when somebody invites you to their birthday party, you don't refuse the invitation, because there may not be another such opportunity. As for me, between running around taking care of you, my job, your school the doctor and the specialist, I neglected my friends. They've all evaporated like soap bubbles. So, as I say, I'd like to have all sorts of things, but all I have right now are damned problems."

I told her that I had problems too. Everybody does. That's what Auntie Lilia says. Some have more, others less. Some people are born with problems, like me…

"Yes, and some people are born with a silver spoon in their mouth. What would you say is your biggest problem, my special little biscuit?" she asked.

I looked down at the floor, and, without giving it much thought, said:

"My feet."

"Your feet? Why your feet? What about school, dad, religious studies…no problem?"

"Religious studies? Why religious studies?" Now it was my turn to be surprised.

"Well, because you and I are constantly wrangling over it and I have threatened to forbid you from going."

I shook my head and said: "You like to exaggerate when…you're angry."

"I'm sorry? Does that mean that you've learned how to read me? That you can read your mum? Bravo!"

I didn't read her at all because these are not things you read, they are things you hear, so I just smiled to let her know that, yes, that's what it was, more or less.

"Now, as for your dad, I want to hear your opinion, I'm really interested, would you like, say, for Igor to become your dad?"

The expression on my face must have been terribly funny or awfully stupid, because as soon as she saw it she began to laugh. I quickly shook my head, thinking: and what's wrong with Professor Nikola? Could I choose? Because what was it with her? Why did she keep choosing such bad house-sitters and dads for me…? I'd more than once imagined Professor Nikola as my dad, his hand running through my hair, but I didn't dare say his name anymore. I didn't want to hear her say: Do you know what the words never again mean? So I kept shaking my head to make it clear what I thought of her suggestion.

"Alright. Calm down. I wouldn't either! Forget that I asked. Actually, it was a stupid idea he had about the three of us, one I simply couldn't agree with," she said, brushing her hair again.

I thought: and what would happen if Professor Nikola had a similar idea about the three of us? Would she have agreed? Would I have found out about it? I remembered that when I was in the corridor listening to their conversation, I'd heard Igor suggest something similar, though it's silly to suggest something you already have. Like children and the fact that you're already somebody's dad. And who needs a double dad? Also, hadn't mum told him that I already had a dad? Except it wasn't yet time for us to talk about it, so I had to wait until I grew up because it was complicated.

How much more would I have to grow, I wondered. How many centimetres? More and more I thought that it would never happen. Because of my feet. That was the problem. I wasn't growing. I was the smallest in my class even though everybody knew that I was the oldest. Tonko once said: "Look at yourself, you're the oldest and the dumbest: the oldest, but a dwarf!" I didn't grow a single centimetre this year. I asked her again if I could lay my ear on her tummy. Maybe I'd made a mistake. Maybe my hearing had been off that day.

"It wasn't, Emil. We both know it wasn't. The fact is that the baby had to go. It's gone…"

"Where?"

"Emil, I'll be late for work, I really don't have time for explanations and more questions. Anyway, my tummy hurts and I've got cramps. Because of the baby that's gone; everything hurts. That sound you heard was swallowed up by the dark."

"You mean like when objects are swallowed up by the night?"

She was silent at first, then she nodded and said: "Something like that."

Her mobile rang. It said *Nikola* …

It rang again. It said *Igor*…

She pretended she hadn't seen or heard anything. Then she got a text message. First one, then another. Again no reaction. She fixed her hair in front of the mirror, put on some lipstick and might have been waiting for me to ask some more questions. Or not waiting for anything. I wasn't either, but I felt like talking. That sometimes happens. Mum says it's increasingly happening at the wrong time and in the wrong place. Like now.

"You still haven't told me the story about the dog."

"What dog?" she asked, opening her eyes wide to put on mascara in front of the mirror.

"The one whose eyes you stung with pepper when you were little and naughty."

"Hah! You certainly choose your moments. I'll tell you the story later, when we come home from the play. Right now, I'm in a hurry. I don't like being late for work, though, as things stand now, I almost don't care. Even if the issue of being fired is raised, I don't care anymore. You know, and this is something I haven't told anybody, not even Zrinka or Jakov, I've got a new job in the works, I'm just waiting for the final confirmation before telling Igor next week: 'Fuck you and your stall, and all that New Year kitsch, and the cold that's done in my bones, lungs and nerves and…' not to mention everything else. Look, they say it's not nice to bite the hand that feeds you, whatever it's like, but I suppose I can allow myself to vent now and then."

"He said he loves you."

"You could stop eavesdropping, you know? It's rude. Don't think that just because you can hear everything, you understand things that concern grown-ups!"

"He wasn't lying."

"So now you even know when somebody's lying?" She looked at me in the mirror with a raised eyebrow, like Instantly when he looked at me in the rear-view mirror of his car.

"Maybe. Unless I misheard..."

"Emil, listen to me! Grown-ups sometimes do stupid things, and then they say things that are even stupider than what they did. It has nothing to do with the truth. Don't fall for every piece of nonsense that you hear and decode in your abstract way."

"What nonsense? How can telling you that I love you be ab-stract!"

"It's absolutely not the same thing if you tell me or if he tells me! You're one thing, he's something completely different! Actually, he's nothing! But you're everything to me! Listen, I just remembered, you haven't told me about the secret connection between me and the fountain in the courtyard. Huh? Where did you get that idea?"

She changed the subject so quickly that I couldn't keep up. And it hadn't been an idea, it's what I'd heard. Because everything has a sound to it. Everything makes a noise. Even when it seems quiet and still. But there couldn't have been a worse moment to talk about it, because we were just on our way out. She to work and I to school. Anyway, it was too complicated for me to explain. It was easier to say everything with modelling clay than to explain the already explained with words. So, I said that she hadn't told me her story about the dog and pepper either, because I could never choose the right time. A moment that was good for us both to trade stories. If she agreed...

She looked at me quietly in the mirror, squinting her eyes, an enigmatic smile on her face. Finally, she nodded her head and said:

"Alright. The story about the dog in exchange for the story about the fountain. Although it looks a bit as if you're blackmailing your own mother, but I think it's more that you're beginning to learn how the grown-up world works..."

She then went back to putting on her make-up and I switched to another subject, because we seemed to have finished with this one:

"What's the new job you've found?"

"It's in a boutique. But let's not talk about it now. Why are you so chatty all of a sudden? You'll be late for school. Is your schoolbag ready? Stop following me around, bombarding me with questions..."

My schoolbag had been ready for ages, the books were in their place. I shoved Instantly's things into the two side pockets that served no purpose and that I never used. It wasn't easy to open them. They had a strong clasp and a small hole and it took me all afternoon to open them, push everything inside and close them again. It was harder than lacing my shoes. I'd promised to be the temporary guardian of his packets that risked being stolen from him. That's why he couldn't keep them himself. He didn't believe anybody anymore. He had no friends (neither did mum). The life he lived made it hard to keep real friends. Some had left on one-way tickets. (!?) Others had turned into snitches (Like Judas?) And as for enemies, they bred like cats. Before you knew it, you'd have a litter in front of you. That's how it was in his line of business. It wasn't simple like selling little cribs and little fir trees.

I knew that mum would agree with him on almost every count: friends, little fir trees, little cribs, God, money...It struck me more and more that if those two ever met they would agree on lots of things. Everybody was looking to grass on him, he said. Well, I wouldn't. He knew I wouldn't. He had a good feel for people. And he knew I was a good person. I could have grassed on him a hundred times by now, but I hadn't.

"And you won't, will you, kid?" he said, eying me in the rear-view mirror. I shook my head, of course I wouldn't. As the bakery receded into the muddy pools in the distance, I asked:

"Where are…the tiles?"

"What tiles?"

"The Italian tiles."

His explosion of laughter sounded like those screeching black birds. But it quickly turned into a cough. He coughed so violently that I thought he would choke. He didn't say another word. Until he parked in the shade of the old oak trees.

"Be a good kid. Not a word to anybody. It was a little secret that first time, but now it's a big secret. Friends keep their secrets. And I believe in you, kid! Do this and I'll repay you! If there's something you want, tell me right now and I'll take care of it. What do you want more than anything else in the world? OK, how much dosh do you want? Blurt out a figure…"

I shook my head.

"You don't want dosh? You really are special! What normal person doesn't want dosh? What do you want then? A watch? A mobile?"

"Most of all I'd like a brother or sister."

"Oh…fuck! That's not the sort of wish I can fulfil! I mean, I can, your old lady is a good piece of ass, but she wouldn't agree to the idea. (She would agree with a lot of things, I'm telling you…) And even if she did, I'd be a bad dad. (He couldn't be worse than the invisible one.) I'm not good for anybody. If you're not good for yourself, how can you be good for anybody else? So, change your wish. You've got time. Think about it."

And so, every day I went back and forth with those little packets. School-home-school-home. Nobody would have even thought of sticking their nose, or nozzle as Instantly would say, into the side pockets of my schoolbag. Not mum, not anybody.

That day, a new surprise awaited us in front of the religious studies room.

The Blessed Mother had disappeared!

The school corridor was full of children who now called it "the site of the disappearance" not the site of the "apparition". There were surprised sighs, whispers, speculations over what had happened. Everybody had question marks hanging over their heads. Even the plastic mountain and vase with artificial flowers were gone. The English teacher's comment was:

"Oh my God! She's disappeared! Is it magic or religion?"

She found it all very funny, and that offended the religious studies teacher. Somebody asked Tonko if he knew what rude thing the English teacher had just said, but he didn't know either, because we hadn't studied English. While we were milling around, wondering what had happened to Our Lady, I heard somebody behind us say that she was inside. In the wall! The director had had her walled up? I thought I would faint with shock! My legs felt like two soft gum drops.

"But how...can she breathe?" I said, I who never said anything. Unless they asked me. And even then, rarely. I didn't think what I said was funny, but naturally everybody else did. What would have happened if Tonko hadn't said:

"Imbecile, it's just a sculpture! How can a sculpture breathe?"

"But it's not just a sculpture, Tonko! That's not what I taught you children," the still-offended religion teacher leapt to my defence. "This is merely a temporary measure, until we decide what to do and how to resolve this dispute."

Later in class, the teacher told us that the trouble caused by this problem had only just begun. The next step would be a petition (?!) where parents would declare themselves "for" or "against" bringing the sculpture of Our Lady into the school. My mum would certainly be against it, I knew that in advance, even without the petition. As usual, nobody was going to ask me for my opinion.

I'd noticed that lately the teacher often ran her hand over that second heart. As if protecting it from something. From somebody making a sudden move, for instance, or something like that. And she was probably good at it because the sound was still there. It hadn't gone away or been swallowed up by the dark. It was nice to hear it though I pretended not to hear anything. I was afraid that she might ask me if I'd asked mum how babies come into the tummy. Then I'd have to tell her what mum had said. And that would have ended badly because I'd have had to mention what mum had said about her tummy and Professor Nikola.

The whole time I watched the sky, thinking about the weather forecast. It had said – possibility of snow! Who wouldn't look forward to that!

At the end of the last lesson, we pushed the school benches back against the wall, and then the parents started arriving. I waved at mum as soon as she walked in. She blew me a kiss and sat down on the back bench. She looked beautiful. She was the prettiest mum in the whole class. At least I thought so. Maybe everybody thinks that their mum is the prettiest because they love her. And whatever you love can only be beautiful.

The play started and everybody in it had changed into their costumes. Everybody except me. I realized that nothing would come of my part that required me to sit under the fir tree and play the fool. I mean, the gift. Either the teacher had forgotten about me or else she'd made the decision at the last minute. I wasn't sorry. Not at all! But I couldn't stop thinking about mum on the back bench.

She was sitting, watching, listening and wondering when was it going to be my turn? How much longer would she have to wait? Until the very end?

Meanwhile, I sat on the school bench, wringing my hands. I didn't have to turn around and look at her to know that mum looked more and more like the fountain in our courtyard. On the outside, she was still the same, but on the inside? A flood…

The play came to an end forty-five minutes later, and that was to be followed by refreshments and snacks. That same moment I could feel mum! A kind of tingling feeling. A kind of gentle prickling in the neck. Kind of like her hand in my hair. Or maybe she felt me and how I kept thinking about her. It could have been that as well. Anyway, our thoughts overlapped, like the hands of a clock and that's when I turned around. We wished the same thing: to leave the classroom that minute and get far away from this place where we did not belong. I realized, or maybe it just occurred to me, that you can be in a place, as I was now, but not belong to it. It was simple. You didn't belong and that was that. Full stop. The end.

She rose to her feet and walked over to me.

"Where's your jacket?" she asked, her bottom lip trembling.

I pointed at the hanger.

The teacher was surprised and opened her mouth to say something, but mum beat her to it:

"The play was…unforgettable! Thank you for the effort you made to give Emil a part. It was very, very…" she searched for the right word, "especially educative!"

The teacher opened her mouth again, but was even quicker to close it. Then she opened it again. Nothing came out except for the air whistling through her teeth. But her hearts! They both leapt as if they were about to fly out. Onto the parquet. Right here in front of everybody. And all the parents and children were quiet now. Only mum could be heard. I looked at the floor as we walked to the door, counting my steps, those *clomp-clomp* noises trailing behind us.

The door slammed shut! Like the one at home which sometimes slams. Except here, instead of my Smurf, there was the sculpture in the wall. Like a silent observer. I wondered if it had fallen onto its back. Could objects, like people, sometimes fall un-conscience? Because who can say for sure that they don't hear and don't breathe just because they are silent and don't move? But I couldn't hear anything on the other side of the wall, even though I strained my ears.

Which didn't necessarily mean that stars, boxes, Smurfs, sculptures, benches, walls, stairs…didn't hear or breathe, even if people thought they didn't. Like me: I have very good hearing, but everybody thinks otherwise.

We walked down the corridor without saying a word, holding hands as we went down the stairs. And at that moment, it started to…

snow…

snow…

snow…

I didn't see it, but I heard it! It was everywhere, it was falling on the city. It was coming down! Rustling! Singing! Dancing like a big flock of white butterflies. I thought then of something so impossible that I knew I couldn't tell anybody. Not mum! Not Instantly! Not anybody! Just me. I had the crazy feeling that this was happening because of me. That it was snowing because I had so wanted it to. I had wanted it so badly that it wasn't normal! And that's why it happened. It improved my mood a little. But not mum's.

The lock on the door of the Ford had frozen. She swore to herself, she swore at the lock, and at the snow, and at the teacher, she pushed and jiggled the key this way and that. Meanwhile, the snow was already sticking to the branches, the grass, the road, the ground, the street lamp, my hair, and my special shoes. Yes, even they looked different, magical, unreal… I stuck out my tongue, closed my eyes and let the snow melt in my mouth. Until I heard:

"Get in. Buckle up."

I sat down on the back seat and we drove off. We didn't say a word about what had happened in the classroom, because there was nothing to say. So maybe it was a good thing that she started with what interested both of us:

"Which story shall we hear first, the one about the fountain or the one about the dog and the pepper? How about you start? I assume your story is lighter than mine…"

"Lighter?"

"When you hear mine, you'll know what I mean. I wish I had never mentioned it. But since I did, and you insist on hearing it, I can't take it back. You first…"

I swallowed my saliva and settled into my seat because it wasn't easy for me either to explain what the modelling clay had already explained. So I began to talk, slowly, as best I could, about the water, about the flood and the tears that flowed backwards. Like the fountain in our courtyard, whose spray mechanism didn't work.

"That's like you, mum…your crying mechanism doesn't work."

She repeated *crying mechanism* a few times. Then she started to explain, more to herself than to me, that obviously, many of her mechanisms weren't working. And that if she could turn back the clock, she thought she would still use the same *faulty* mechanisms. Because that's the sort of material she was made of, unlike her sister, all of whose mechanisms, including her defence mechanism, worked perfectly…

"You know Emil, my story begins with the fact that I didn't have a dad when I was little either."

"?!"

"You see, we carry childhood traumas like holes, like hollows where memories sometimes surface. My mum, your grandmother, raised us on her own. And there was a man who lived in our street and he had a dog. Not a day passed by that he didn't tease my sister and me, bombarding us with jokes about orphans and self-supporting women. One day he asked me to walk his dog. I agreed and concocted a plan. I knew the dog wasn't to blame, but I had to bare my teeth somehow! I don't know myself how I thought of the pepper. I put a muzzle on him, opened the bag of pepper and spilled it out. The dog went crazy. Reeling and sneezing, he finished up on the bridge and fell straight into the sea. It was winter. When I stood at his owner's door a little later, I explained what had happened. I didn't mention the pepper. He asked me if I thought he looked retarded. What did I mean the dog drowned? All dogs know how to swim. Why was I lying? He threatened me and said he would take me to court. Me and mum, together. That he would drown us like cats. He said that my dad had been clever to leave us. That I had killed his dog, and I would have killed my dad too if he'd just given me enough time. This went on and on until mum wrote him a letter and put it in his letterbox. The letter went something like this: 'People who find themselves on the margins of life are people who were driven beyond those margins in their own home. They stuff their pockets with stones, because there is nobody to help them remove the stones inside them. Death is setting off from, journeying from, leaving one shore in order to reach another, perhaps better shore. These are not my words they are the words of your wife, which she left in my letterbox the day she jumped off that same bridge. I don't know whom you are angry at, but I won't let you take it out on us, because I know something about your private life. So stop. It's not nice when ghosts from the past run our lives.'

And that's that, Emil. I never forgot that dog. Sometimes I dream about it. And I never forgot the spanking my mum gave me because of it. After that, the man stopped threatening to sue us and telling rude jokes about us. He moved away and I never saw him again. It's a sad story, you see..."

"..."

"You have nothing to say?"

"..."

"Alright, then we're done with that. Let's go for a drive and then head home..."

The story was so sad that I didn't even manage to nod my head. I could barely breathe. I wanted to cry so badly, because of...what I had told her, and because of what she had told me and because of what should have happened in the classroom during the play but didn't. I wanted to go home and had no idea why we were still driving around. We should have reached home a long time ago. But how could we reach home when we were still driving aimlessly around town. I didn't dare ask what the plan was. It seemed we were without a plan. Now that we had told our stories, it was as if we were ashamed of them, as if it would have been better if we didn't even know about them. At least that's how it seemed to me.

At one point we ran a red light. At another the car skidded. Then the town was behind us. Only a snowy dense forest and an empty road lay ahead of us. Then there was nothing. The darkness swallowed up everything except for our faces. I buried my head in the seat and pretended to sleep. I pretended that crying was the furthest thing from my mind. And I especially pretended not to see her face and that... her *crying mechanism* was working. But I was never good at pretending with mum. The last thing I remember was:

"Emil, don't cry. We're going home. Everything will be OK."

Paper Dragon

NOTHING WAS OK. We didn't get home. Mum was nowhere to be seen. This time she didn't show up in the evening, or the next day, or the day after the next day, she didn't show up at all. When I came to on the tenth day, I mean my tenth finger, I stopped counting. The days passed by but still she didn't come. The room I slept in had three equally white beds. From one of them I looked every day at the big sunlit windows. Nothing was left of the snow, not even the smallest trace of white.

The saliva in my mouth tasted of medicine and of that liquid cleaning ladies use to wash the floor twice a day. Plus, I vomited. Not because of that, but because of the concussion, a shock to the brain. I heard them say that was the reason. I still thought it was all because of mum. Because I couldn't understand how the brain could be shocked. And what did the stomach and mouth have to do with it? It was more likely to be the heart. It flapped inside me like the wings of a frightened bird. But nobody mentioned the heart, and nobody checked it the way they did the other parts of my body. If they had, some machine would have surely shown them why I was vomiting and crying all the time. And that it was because mum wasn't there, and I didn't know how to be on my own. They kept saying that I had been lucky, unlike mum who hadn't been lucky, and that a concussion, broken wrist and a few bruises were nothing. I would recover. I was young.

But I thought that if it really was about my brain, maybe it would be normal if it made me smarter, or the opposite – stupider. But none of that happened. I could still count properly only up to ten. Except I had become even quieter. But I didn't think that had anything to do with the brain, it was more to do with the tongue. Nobody paid any attention to it because everybody knew that I wasn't chatty even at the best of times. But I knew that if she were here, mum would have been displeased. Because she made sure that I kept up with my social skills.

As for my hearing, nothing had changed. That became clear once the dizziness and vomiting stopped. I'd say that it became even sharper than before. In the hospital I realized that I could write a book, if I were somebody else, somebody like Emil and Tonko combined, with *my hearing and his imagination*! Because all sorts of people walked down those hospital corridors. All sorts of people lay in bed on the other side of the wall. I heard all sorts of things, including things I *didn't want* to hear. I could have written a big fat book of...I don't how many pages. But I wasn't Tonko. And I wouldn't be writing anything. Because maybe it wasn't that important to write about strangers. To poke one's nose into other people's business. Because maybe somebody might one day poke their nose into our business, mum's and mine. And who knew what kind of story that would make. Because not everybody has the same eyes for seeing and the same ears for listening.

In the hospital I slept a lot and I dreamt a lot. Mostly about mum. Us driving in the Ford. Mum and me. Sometimes it was also in Instantly's Audi. I knew that because it smelled of sweets. We were driving somewhere; we had a long trip ahead of us and the road was flat and outside the window I could see the dense woods and the falling snow. She was silent while we sped down the road. At some point before we reached our destination, mum opened her mouth as if to say something, but she couldn't. A flash of sunlight jolted me awake. And that was the end of it. Mum stayed on one side of the dream and I on the other. I had the same dream more than once, but the end was always the same. Like an unfinished story. There are stories like that as well, the teacher said. That meant: nothing was finished, even when it looked as if it was.

At first, I refused to eat the hospital food. Not because it was hospital food and smelled of chemicals and medicines, but because it wasn't served on the plate the way I like it, in small morsels and with blue Smurf toothpicks. I also refused to get out of my hospital bed. Again, not because I didn't like it, but because I kept trying, in every way I knew how, to get back to the dream I kept losing. I'd pull the blanket over my head and press my closed eyes. Until it hurt. I thought that if I pressed hard enough, I'd get back into my dream. Because what if mum managed to say something in my dream? What if she said: "Emil, I love you!" or hugged me and said: "Biscuit, everything will be OK"?

But most of all I wanted to be there because even in my dream I could smell her hair.

I don't know how many days passed by before I stopped crying, calling out for her, talking. I mean, aloud. But anybody with an ear that was any good could hear that I was still doing it inside me, and that I hadn't grown *stronger,* which was what they interpreted my dry eyes and empty mouth to mean. And then the dreams went away as well.

They became empty. Like empty beds waiting for their occupants. Like a TV set without picture or sound. Like a mouth without words. The only thing that got stronger was the mixture of sounds around. Plugging my ears didn't help. It was the same with my eyes, which made me think that dreaming had nothing to do with closing your eyes, just as my hearing had nothing to do with plugging my ears.

The sounds kept following me. Like the faithful dog I never had. They would spread over me the way the shadows spill over objects in the room at night.

"Emil, remember what we learned in religious studies, that souls go to heaven and eternal bliss...," the religion teacher said when she visited me one day and stood by my bed next to the other visitors.

"I'm sure that she's now with...the angels...," to which *It's Good to Do Good* said:

"Stop confusing him with angels here, heaven there. He didn't even attend religious studies properly, so I don't understand why you are using such terminology. He needs to be told what really happened, not misled with fairy tales!"

The other teacher said: "Look, you're the last person in the world who should be lecturing anybody! If it were up to me, I would have you suspended! It's enough to remember the school play. And let's not forget that little incident when you nonchalantly went off to the museum!" The religion teacher was ready with her answer: "What do you want to say, that our religion is a fairy tale?"

"I want to say...I want to say...," the other teacher stammered. "That you could stoop this low, I have no words. To accuse me so pathetically like this! You haven't a clue what you're talking about, you weren't there that day in the classroom, but still, you like engaging in idle gossip from the school corridors. Everything I did was with the best of intentions."

"The road to hell is paved with good intentions too...," replied the religion teacher, looking away.

"Stop already with the hypocrisy! I wanted to say that if you can't find the right words to console him, then leave him be, because his mum didn't support that ideology, and that should be respected. Emil, listen to me...," she turned to me, "do you understand what happened to your mother?"

I nodded and said yes, but that I'd forgotten what we were given for homework. What was the last subject we had? Where did we stop? I didn't have any modelling clay or wooden pencils here...

"For heaven's sake, Emil!" the shocked teacher said, placing her hand on her upper heart. "I didn't come here because of homework, grades or modelling clay. (What then?) Forget that. It's not at all important. (Why isn't it, suddenly?) What's important is that you recover. (I wish mum had recovered too.) I just came to see if you were alright. (Even a blind man could see that I'm not.) All your classmates send their best and are waiting for you to come back to your school desk. (That sounds like a lie.) I'm asking you; do you understand what happened to your mother?"

"Yes. She went...home."

"No, Emil. Mum did not go home...she died."

"And Professor Antun went too."

"Who? Where did he go?"

"Home."

"You don't understand," Miss Vjeka stepped in. "He's talking about our late neighbour. I don't know why Emil is mentioning him now. He died recently. At home. That's probably what he meant. Emil, is that what you meant?"

Of course not. I never mean what other people think I mean. And since none of them had heard the story of people and stars, I decided not to say anything.

Auntie Zrinka and Uncle Jakov came every day. They brought presents and lots of sweets. But they never thought of bringing plain gum drops. Or mum's apple pie. Even a shoebox would have been enough. The paper dragon, the one from China, was still in one of those boxes at home. The dragon that never flew, though that had nothing to do with the wind. Though it would have been easy to blame the weather for the fact that it never once managed to fly.

So I asked them if there wasn't maybe a new dragon among the new presents?

"Certainly not!" Uncle Jakov immediately said. "You've got nothing to be afraid of, Emil. No dragons or monsters. Just toys and Lego building blocks. Go on, open them! You'll like them."

They didn't know, for instance, that a dragon doesn't use its feet to get around. That's why it has such big wings. Like butterflies. Birds. Ladybirds. Maybe they do know, but they don't think about feet, because their feet are as firmly on the ground as grass. As Professor Antun would say: "People are like blades of grass; they spend their lives growing deep roots in order to counter the force of the wind, which means they miss the opportunity to…," I don't know exactly what, but it was something to do with a different way of getting around. A dragon doesn't have such problems. All it needs is the wind in its wings. It touches the ground only to spew fire out of its mouth or smoke out of its ears, and then it flies away. If it were true that I was special, as I've always been told, then what I want, my wish, would come true. Even flying to the stars wouldn't seem impossible.

But there I was, still lying in bed, listening to the howling wind on the other side of the window, and to the two of them talking about some time in the future when we'd spend time together and go on outings. I'd never heard their promises creak so clearly before. There was no chance that anything would come of them because that's just something people say: *one day we'll go to*...And if you don't do something right away, but just talk and talk about it, that's what it remains. Talk.

Then I remembered their child. I asked if it had already arrived.

"Excuse me? What are you talking about? What child?" Auntie Zrinka went stiff and immediately stepped in. "And how do you know about it?"

There were two possibilities: I could say that I knew because I had heard everything, through closed doors, through the walls of the room, through the walls of their bodies. Or I could say nothing. I chose the latter and just kept staring at her. Maybe that's why she turned away to look out the window.

"It arrived yesterday," Uncle Jakov replied in her place. "It's a boy, but we haven't given him a name yet. I hope you will have a chance to meet him."

And there the conversation somehow ended, because Auntie Zrinka kept looking out the window even though there was nothing to see except for the sky, the clouds and the occasional flock of birds. So Uncle Jakov didn't say anything more either. As for me, I didn't have enough air again. That had started happening ever since the school play. I got out of bed and opened the window. I breathed in and out. And again I thought that it was enough to wish very hard for the impossible; to make the room disappear, or me disappear before their eyes, or to fly away like the dragon or Peter Pan, just as I had once wished for snow and it had come. After that maybe I wouldn't have at all minded to hear somebody say: "We always said that he was special, and not just because of his shoes." The way they once said about Jesus: "This man truly was the son of God." Although they kept telling him till the end that he was ordinary, the most ordinary of men. Nothing special.

But nothing happened. I didn't specially disappear in front of their eyes. By the time people realized Jesus was special it was too late. By then they'd already nailed him to the tree like a common thief.

And here in the room, the two of them hunched their shoulders when I opened the window.

"Emil, it's cold," I head Auntie Zrinka say. "Shut the window. We'll freeze."

Their teeth chattered, and that wasn't all that shivered before they left, saying that they'd be back tomorrow.

"Is there anything you'd like or wish for?" they asked at the door.

I shook my head. They didn't know anything about my very ordinary wishes: gum drops, apple pie and a shoebox.

When I left the hospital and returned to the flat, I found it cold and deserted. Colourless. Soundless. Solitude had a special smell: the smell of dried flowers in a vase and a mouldy cake forgotten on the table. Although Auntie Zrinka, Miss Dunja and another lady whose name I didn't know were sitting in the kitchen, loneliness clung to all the objects in the flat. I lacked air as I looked at the things around me. They were just as we had left them that day. That's why they looked so strange and unreal. As if mum might poke her head around any minute and say: "Here I am, my special little biscuit, come…come…come…"

The mascara brush was still lying on the glass shelf in the bathroom. Dirty dishes peered out of the sink. Our clothes hung over the edge of the bed. Waiting for us in the hallway were mum's slippers, and my toppled Smurf by the phone. I let him lie there in his un-conscience world. I buried my face in her pillow. It still smelled of her, but this wasn't a dream. How was it possible that everything smelled of mum? Both in my dreams and in real life. And yet she was gone, gone…

I was lying there like that when suddenly the parquet creaked. Right at the spot where it always does when somebody steps on it. Except there was nobody. Just the air. The same thing happened in front of the wardrobe. And the third time in front of the big mirror. And then the curtains moved, as if from a breeze. And something like a breath gently lifted the hair off my brow. OK, maybe I imagined it all. Maybe I just had a huge desire for something to be there where there was nothing. Then again, who can say that it wasn't as I thought.

I heard Auntie Zrinka say from the kitchen that I should close the window. There was a draught. We would all freeze. Then she lowered her voice and said:

"Now do you see? He's sure to have some disorder that's connected with his body temperature. Or an obsession with windows and air. Even in the hospital he would fling open the windows and stay quiet, as he does, he'd just look at you without saying a word. That's what I find the hardest, when he just looks at me with that fixed stare and says nothing. Who knows what he's thinking at that moment, maybe he isn't thinking at all. Marina didn't mention any disorders other than the ones he already has. I'm not really surprised, it's natural for parents to hide their child's faults and shortcomings from the rest of the world. But from your own sister? I have to be honest, maybe it was because I didn't have the best relationship with her. I was her older sister and I didn't approve of anything she did."

That's when I noticed that I couldn't see my schoolbag anywhere. Not in my room, and not in the hallway. I didn't want to go to the kitchen and ask about it because all those ladies were still there. So I decided to wait until they left. Though, when I thought about it, I didn't know why I needed it. Who, except for mum, would want to know what homework I had? Who, except for Instantly, would want to know if everything was in a safe place? And right now, Instantly seemed incredibly far away. Like a parallel line that would never meet up with my own line again.

Out in the road, cars rumbled by, and here in the room, different sounds were coming in through the walls, the sounds of talking, coughing, laughter, water left in the pipes, the lift opening and closing, footsteps big and small…And it didn't stop, the way at first I thought it would. Nothing stopped except for me.

I still hurt all over, but I wasn't sure if it was from the accident or something else. Because how could you explain the pain of inhaled air in your lungs, of eaten food in your tummy, of walking in your legs.

In the kitchen, they were still talking.

"Look, unfortunately...I don't feel that I'm up to it, what you're asking is too much for me."

"You are his closest relative..."

"Listen, my husband and I...we have a child to take care of now. I've told you all about it. I told you that I never established a good relationship with Emil. Actually, no relationship at all..."

"You always manage. Think it over. You'd get all the help you need from the relevant institutions..."

"It's not a question of money or institutions. I still maintain that somebody born with special needs should have appropriate care on a permanent, not an ad hoc basis. I'm not a nurse or a special education teacher, or a psychologist, and I'm not a mother either, I don't know anything about children. Marina once said something similar after we had a fight: 'You haven't a clue about children, you don't understand a thing. You'll talk differently when you have children of your own.' And you see, since I still haven't got children of my own, my view of the problem remains unchanged. That's why I'm not prepared to do this. I'm sorry, but I feel too much pressure is being placed on me and I can't make the right decision under pressure."

"Think it over another day or two. From what I hear, your husband would be willing. He seems to have become fond of the boy, but he says it all depends on you. He's left it for you to decide."

"That's best. My decision, my responsibility. He spends most of his time on business trips and doesn't know anything about raising a child, especially not in this specific situation. He doesn't know how he will manage with his own child. To be clear, I have absolutely no doubt about his good intentions, but that's simply not enough. It's not enough and in the end, I'd be left to cope with it all on my own. I simply don't want to take on something I'm not sure I'll be able to carry through. If Marina were here, I'm sure she'd say that I always played it safe in life and never took any risks. And she'd be right. That's why I am where I am, and she's..." She didn't finish because there was the sound of crying, and sniffling, and soothing words and...

Then the doorbell rang.

"Good afternoon. Is Emil here? I wanted to see him and say hello, if I'm not bothering anybody..." It was the voice of Miss Vjeka. I'd stopped calling her *It's Good to Do Good* even in my mind.

Auntie Zrinka knocked at my door and asked if I was up for a visit. If not, she'd easily get rid of the tiresome woman.

I nodded my head.

A surprise meowed in her arms! A little white ball that I immediately reached out to with the hand that wasn't in a cast. I liked its warmth and softness and its sad meowing. My own sadness was eased by this feeling that there was someone lonelier than me. That I wasn't the only one missing his mum.

"He's yours if you want him. He has nobody. He's looking for an owner and I thought of you. You've always been fond of cats. And they of you. Do you want him?"

I nodded.

"Think of a name for him. Do you have any in mind?

I shrugged. But then it came to me! Snowflake! He was white. Like a big flake of snow that had fallen out of the sky right into my lap.

"I hear that you'll be here for a few more days and then you're leaving. I wanted to ask you, that's to say I brought you a small picture of a saint, the patron saint of children. If you want it. I don't want you to think that I'm insisting or pushing anything on you, as your teacher says. I just wish you well, Emil..."

Well, alright then, the old picture had fallen apart in my schoolbag anyway. The schoolbag that had disappeared.

"Wherever you are, I'll think of you. You'll be in all my prayers. If you move to another town and I'm in the area, I'll come and see you. OK?"

What other town?

"Do you know that somebody broke into your flat? You don't? A few days after the...accident. I had just come back from mass when I saw that your front door was open. I immediately called the police, but your aunt says that she doesn't think anything was stolen. It's all a bit strange, if you ask me. A break-in, and nothing missing! They weren't forthcoming with information, so that's all I can tell you."

As soon as everyone left, and the two of us were on our own, I asked Auntie Zrinka about the break-in.

"Yes, it's true, but I don't know why that woman had to tell you about it. To upset you even more. I'm sorry now that I didn't slam the door in her face. The police called and wanted me to come and see if anything was missing, but it all looked fine to me. There wasn't even a mess, except for the one you left behind you. I don't know what to think about it."

"My bag...isn't here."

"What bag? Your schoolbag? Hmm, I forgot about that. But listen, it's impossible to think that somebody would break in to the flat just for your schoolbooks. Why would anybody need them?"

"It's not here."

"I have a clear recollection of when they brought me the things from…from…the wrecked car, I took the bag and put it in your room. I don't know where it could have gone. Unless Vjeka was nosing around the place after she discovered the door was open and before the police came. Marina used to say that that woman liked poking her nose into other people's business, so nothing would surprise me."

I said that I would look around the room some more, even though I knew there was nothing to see there. You can walk around my room in just a few steps. The only two places I hadn't checked yet was under my bed and in the wardrobe where my boxes were.

Naturally, I didn't find it, but I immediately realized that somebody had been touching my boxes, that they weren't stacked as they should be. It was pretty much a mess, so I started putting everything back in order. The kite had been in the bottom, biggest box but now that box was on top. It wasn't closed properly so I tried to see what the problem was. That's how I found a sticky paper between the dragon's wings. With writing on it. It was written in big block letters and it was about me. Because I'm the only *Kid* there is. And there was only one person who called me – *Kid*.

KID!

FUCK IT. I'M PROPER SORRY ABOUT YOUR OLD LADY. I SAW THE DEATH NOTICE DOWNSTAIRS ON THE DOOR. IF YOU'RE READING THIS THEN YOU KNOW THAT I PICKED UP MY STUFF. I LOOKED FOR THE OTHER THING BUT DIDN'T

FIND IT. I FORGIVE YOU BECAUSE OF THE SHIT YOU'VE BEEN THROUGH WITH YOUR OLD LADY. FOR A LONG TIME I WAS IN A BAD WAY MYSELF AFTER MINE LEFT. STAY STRONG AND BE CLEVER. AND DON'T HAVE ANYTHING TO DO WITH SCUMBAGS ANYMORE. I TOLD YOU THAT I'M NO GOOD FOR ANYBODY. I HOPE NOBODY EXCEPT YOU WILL STICK THEIR NOZZLE INTO THESE FUCKING SHOE BOXES.

PS: THROW THIS PAPER INTO THE SHIT HOLE WHEN YOU FINISH READING IT!

And the shit hole was what? The wheelie bin? That's where it really stank. I went to the kitchen and told Auntie Zrinka that I wanted to take out the rubbish. I didn't want to really. You can't start liking smelly things, but I had to get rid of that scrap of paper.

"There's no need. I'll do it. Your arm is in a cast, it's better if you go and lie down..."

I stamped my foot on the floor and repeated what I wanted to do!

"Alright. If you insist. We're not going to fight over the rubbish. Go ahead, take it out."

I grabbed the bag, opened the door and headed for the lift. There was nobody to call after me: "Come back and put your shoes on!" Nobody to say: "Emil, practicing lacing your shoes is for your own good." I don't know, suddenly I desperately missed words I'd never liked hearing. Auntie Zrinka didn't know what was and what wasn't important for me to do. Or how hard I had to work at my social skills. Because there was always the chance that I might run into somebody downstairs who might say: "Good morning! How are you?" And then I'd have to answer, even though I still didn't understand how these greetings work. This time I didn't run into anybody in the hallway and I didn't hear anything. No sound of clomping followed me. It was all quiet, too quiet, and my footsteps were as soft as a cat's.

As soon as I was outside, I looked up at Miss Vjeka's balcony. When I was sure that she wasn't there, I first tossed the rubbish into the wheelie bin, and only then the scrap of paper. But before that I tore it up into tiny pieces. I turned it into paper snow.

Although I would have liked to keep it as a souvenir. Nobody had ever written me a letter or texted me on my mobile. Still, I did exactly what Instantly had told me to do. He probably knew what was best. For him and for me.

Riding up in the lift, I thought of what Miss Vjeka had said:

"If you move to another town…"

Letter

I'M NOW more than ten years old. So I can't count them on my fingers anymore. I still count like that under my desk. Almost everybody else thinks with their head, I think of numbers with my fingers. And to be 13 means in my case that I'm still something like the number 1, Emil with a drooping head, and still a little like the number 0, because it carries a circle of emptiness on its back the way others carry a backpack full of all sorts of things. Except with time the 0 has turned into the number 3. Its tight circle has spread out and loosened.

Here, where I live now, everything is new and different. I share almost everything with others: the room, meals, birthdays, teachers, sometimes even clothes. It's only words that I share with a chosen few.

I also have new doctors. I've become close to some of them. Not too close, but still, you can't have someone make you special shoes, take imprints of your feet, and not know their name. His name is Uncle Filip. What's new is that nobody has to hold my foot down to get a better imprint anymore. I do it myself. He always laughs and says: "Hold onto that foot, lionheart, or else it'll run off!" And it's like a joke that makes even me laugh.

The person who has replaced Auntie Lilia, is called Auntie Franka. I immediately realized that she'd somehow heard about my fantastic hearing. Although I hadn't said anything to anybody. Although I refuse to admit that I hear better and more than others. Every day we begin or end our talk something like this:

"Emil, yesterday we worked on your speech, and now we'll work a little on your hearing. Tell me, can you hear beyond the sounds inside this room? No? Are you sure? Listen, can you hear any sound at all on the other side of this wall? And what about the window?"

I shake my head no to all her questions.

These last few days she's been asking me this too:

"The other day, when our cook hugged you, you let her do it, you didn't scream or pull back the way you usually do, I mean you don't let even me do that, and we're old friends, you just smiled strangely and didn't move. Can you tell me what happened, did you maybe hear something unusual in her?"

Who wouldn't smile strangely when she's got not two, but three hearts beating inside her!!! It's a good thing I didn't fall un-conscience with surprise. But I told Auntie Franka that I was nothing special, just an ordinary boy, and that nobody normal could hear such things. We weren't in a sci-fi movie.

But she still doesn't believe me. Maybe that's because I never learned to lie well. At least not as well as Tonko. And I guess it shows on my face or can be heard. I don't know.

"I've heard rather different stories about you from the town where you used to live. Auntie Lilia, the teacher Gordana, Professor Nikola – they all say the opposite. What do you have to say to that? It can't be that they're all lying, right?"

And what about the story that the only thing I'm good at is not listening? What about that?

Then she tells me to draw something. Mum, for instance. I draw her exactly as I remember her from the last time I saw her, at the school play, dressed in that same top and trousers, her hair long.

"Good. Now draw snow for me. Or better yet, can you make it out of modelling clay?"

Immediately, with no problems, I make a frozen lake, a little snow-covered house, a snowman…

She shakes her head and wags her finger at me. Again, she doesn't believe me. Because they'd told her that I do it differently. But how can I explain that I don't want people to know what I'm like. Because I don't want to be special! It's hard enough having feet that refuse to be corrected and become just ordinary feet. That's why I play deaf. That's to say, I play naturally deaf, the way everybody around me is naturally deaf.

"The information your school gave me about your artistic and auditory expression is different, so it would have been useful to us now if your former teacher had kept at least one item or drawing as evidence, instead of handing them back as poorly executed homework and grading them accordingly. Now she's claiming she was so over-worked that maybe she was too slow to recognize that you had a certain, specific talent. We'll continue, Emil, we're not done. I think that you're resisting and for some reason don't want to cooperate."

I have to say the following, because it's very important. More important than all that nonsense about hearing and not hearing. Last week I heard from…Professor Nikola!!!

Out of the blue they said: "Emil, you have a call from out of town." How come from out of town, they wondered in surprise, but not before I myself was surprised. For a second, I thought – mum! She's come back! She calling to say that everything's alright! But that was just for a second or two, not more. And then all those people I used to know started popping up in my mind. And when I took the phone and heard his voice, I trembled, my legs immediately turned to jelly. I had to sit down and, as usual, I breathed into the receiver, unable to say a single word. Though I wanted to. I really, really wanted to. I thought that maybe through the phone he would hear my heart beating, my skin growing gooseflesh, my tongue twisting in my mouth, trying to get a word out of the invisible word trap. But he spoke slowly, undisturbed by my silence. I didn't remember a word he said. Except for the part at the end. He had a surprise for me, he said. And no, not because it was a holiday, but because he had never stopped thinking about me. He wasn't sure if I was angry with him because he hadn't been in touch before. He wanted to give everyone time for their wounds to heal. He said that he would write me a letter, because you can't say important things on the phone. You have to look the person in the eye or at least open up your heart on the page, with words. I could reply to his letter If I wanted to, he would like that very much. Because he knew, he'd been informed, that even though I don't talk, I write well and express myself better that way than aloud, which is why he'd like us to exchange our thoughts. About whatever. About the past. About the future. About whatever interests me. About if I'd like him to come and visit me one day? Or maybe I could visit him in our old town?

When he finished the conversation, I held on to the receiver for a long time, as if it were glued to my hand, although you could clearly hear its beep-beep signal. My hand and my ear were warm from the low flame of his words. And then my eyes welled up with tears, and I wiped them away secretly. Because I had never learned how to cry without anyone noticing.

When his letter arrived, it was the second letter – message (counting the one Instantly had attached to the dragon's wing) that I'd ever received in my life. I held it to my chest, unopened, the name of the addressee clearly written on the envelope, until it became limp from my damp hands. For a moment I even thought that I'd be able to read the words and sentences through the envelope, with the help of the skin on my chest, where I'd put it so as not to lose it, that I'd somehow be able to hear, to feel Professor Nikola, even before opening and reading the letter. But I didn't hear anything. Or feel anything. Except myself. And my anxiety.

That's why I needed peace and quiet to open it. And the best place for that was the attic. I always went up there when I wanted to be alone. Or when I wanted to listen to the falling snow. Or when I wanted a book, as there were tons up there. There was no better place than the attic to read, leaf through the pages or listen.

Before I went up, I took a piece of paper and a pencil, so that I could answer his letter right away and wouldn't have to think later about what he had asked me and what I had to say. I didn't want to make a mistake. Or look stupid. Or, even worse, for him to think that I was Emil the imbecile.

It was night-time and everybody was asleep.

As I slipped out of bed, it started to snow. As usual, I didn't see it, but I heard the rustle of it piling up on the rooftops and trees.

There were lots and lots of stairs to climb before reaching the attic. Each time I tried to count them. But incredibly, the number always came out differently. No matter how many times I climbed them, I always finished with a different number. Sometimes I thought that was because the stairs were magical. That it wasn't because I wasn't good at maths. But that the stairs were uncountable. Like the stars in the sky.

The stairs were old and creaked if you walked on them without thinking. But I knew where to step. Maybe Professor Antun would say that I had found the right treble clef for walking silently. I remembered sounds and rustlings the same way other people remembered numbers, names, faces or lessons in nature and social science. I knew exactly where to place my foot, on the outer or inner side of the stair, I knew which stair I needed to skip, and which I should step on exactly in the middle.

When I finally reached the top, the first thing I did was switch on the light and it blazed bright in the little opaque bulb wedged in between the rafters. I could hear the sound of silky rustling and soft fluttering. I opened the roof window and peered out. I opened my mouth, stuck out my tongue and just listened for a while to the icy blobs melting on it, rustling like butterfly wings. They said I could get a sore throat and tonsillitis. Not true. Maybe somebody else could, but not me! It was something I did all the time and I never got sick. Because I've always been like that, healthy. Except for the problem I have with my feet and hands, but they have nothing to do with my health. My tonsils are just fine, except for what happened that once, a long time ago, when I had to stay at home.

I sat down under the window, slowly opened the envelope, took out the sheet of paper and started to read:

My dear Emil,

It's been a long time since we've seen each other and I don't really know where to begin. There've been many changes here since you left, and one of them is that I've changed schools. In the meantime, I got married and now have two children, one from my marriage and one from outside marriage, if you understand what I'm trying to say. One of my boys is named after you. I would like you to meet both of my sons. Bear in mind that the distance dividing us is not very big. It's only a five-hour drive. What do you say about arranging to meet one day?

I immediately started to write my reply on the white sheet of paper so that I wouldn't forget what I wanted to say.

I didn't know anything about marriage, but I knew everything about snowflakes. For instance, it took a snowflake only five minutes to travel from the cloud to the ground, so imagine the distance it had to cover. Not to mention how long it took me to climb up to the attic from the ground floor. About half-an-hour. Sometimes longer because I'd get tired and would have to sit down, then get up, then sit down again…and so on…

I keep going back in my mind to our beginning, when we were trying to devise a physical education programme for you within a school programme that didn't provide even the minimal conditions for such a thing, and when we were thinking of getting you a pair of trainers, but, to my great regret, and I think yours, nothing came of it. That's how it is in life, in some things you succeed, in others you don't. Still, if you sink on one side, you may resurface on another. There are always new paths to be found. One's never too old to learn and I must tell you that I'm at a new beginning again. I've enrolled in another college. I'm back sitting at a school desk – me, an old goat. A father of two. What do you say about the two of us starting from the beginning again as well? Like old friends.

How are your studies and school going?

Maths, forget it, as for the rest I'm not sure. But there are lots of books in the attic. Some of which I read. Some I just leaf through and listen to. I can tell from the amount of dust on them that nobody needs them anymore. One of the books is different from all the others: it's thin and has no cover. It's missing a good part of the beginning because it starts on page 174 with the words "In the beginning was the Word." I sometimes think about all the beginnings that could have happened before the beginning on page 174. How many could there have been? One? Ten? None?

I really hope that the fact that you went to another town and that your mum is gone doesn't mean the end of our relationship. There's always a reason for every person we meet. We shouldn't turn our back on any opportunity. We shouldn't forget the ugly things that have happened, but rather, as with the beautiful ones, we should store them in the album of our memories. That is why I don't want our relationship to end with silence, without giving one another a chance for each to tell his story. You remember the lunch we had together? That's when everything somehow moved towards the end, although I had big plans at the beginning. I mean the end that happened between your mum and me. I hope that we can correct that. You and I. I'd like to explain a few things to you. You're older now, you'll understand...

I often turn to the end of that book. Actually, I go back and forth between the beginning (page 174) and the end.

But I'm drawn to the end because it's exciting and open-ended. That's what you say when you come to the end of a story, but your head is full of questions, even though there's a full stop at the end of the last sentence, and not a single word after that. There's just the whiteness of the paper. Like a mound of snow that's fallen on a bare meadow. I think that means that things could turn out one way or the other. That's how it's often been with me in my life.

I hope you will forgive me for not having believed you back then. But who would have done so in my place? It took time for me to put things together, like the pieces of a puzzle. I remember how shocked I was when you said what you had heard, as if it were the most normal thing in the world to hear the inaudible. I didn't know what to think. Not just because of what it meant you were revealing to us, but because of what I was trying to hide from Marina. You didn't realize it, but your mum did right away...

The end of the book is called Revelation, although how it is going to happen remains hidden. It's in the horsemen of the Apocalypse. And what do you think would happen if I depicted the end of the world like that for my homework? It would be: "Emil, we said depict the end of the world, not depict a barn and farm animals!" To me it's clear as day that the person who wrote the book has special hearing and ears! Like me. Except I'm not a writer. And his ears hear better than mine. Which is why he hears what nobody else hears: how future events are thundering across the land. Sometimes I wonder how things might end if they began with one word? In the mouth? On the tongue? In a morsel? What if God loses his appetite in the end? Because the world is going bad, the way food goes bad. And if everything becomes useless, it turns into a tasteless morsel. Will we be spit out onto some sci-fi rubbish heap waiting to be recycled? Like an old piece of Čunga Lunga chewing gum that you can't make bubbles with anymore…

I'm told, Emil, that you don't want anything for Christmas. That it's like that every year. But I'm positive you haven't given up on a pair of trainers. So, I've decided that my present to you will be a new pair. I don't know what size you wear so please let me know somehow. I keep thinking that after all these years I won't recognise you anymore. That you're completely different now. Taller. Mature. I don't need the people raising you to tell me how sweet and different you are. Even without them I know that we need to love the differences in other people…

I don't know what people are made of, maybe it's mud as they say in *Catechism,* but snowflakes, for instance, are made of crystals. And during the five minutes that it takes for them to come down from the cloud to the ground, their crystals merge with other crystals in the air. That's why you can't predict what form they'll take when they touch the ground. They're not just irregular-looking titbits of ice. They just look like that and trick the eye. Like me: I'm ordinary, as ordinary as can be, while every snowflake is special and different. No two are the same. The possibilities are endless…

Now Emil, I hear that you have breathing problems and asthma? How did that happen?

I don't know. But I do know that it happens because I don't have enough air in my lungs. A bit like with the snowflakes. (There I go, talking about snowflakes again). When they fall onto the ground and create a thick layer, they make a crunching sound if you step on them. That happens because of the air trapped in the layers of snow. When you walk on them it presses out the air...

I hope you are alright now and that you are getting therapy. Take care, maybe you're just allergic to dust...

I'm not. And I can talk about...snowflakes until the cows come home. In the centre of every one of them is a particle of dust - or the dust of creation. And that's not something I invented or thought up, because I'm not like that, no, I read it in a book. But then I wonder, what if the world was created like that? Out of cosmic dust. And I always wonder: if a snowflake knew that it would melt as soon as it fell to the ground, and that even before that somebody might step on it, would it fly away? Or would it give up before flying away?

It took me more than half an hour to climb down from the attic - taking care not to make a noise - to the room where everybody was still asleep, though I could see faint traces of dawn outside the window.

I heard the rustling of snow start to fade.

I dressed. I managed to lace my special shoes on the first go. I waited for the first sounds of movement on the ground floor. Nothing happened for a long, long time. Or else I was just impatient. And when you're impatient, time slows down. In the end, I decided that there was no way I would give my letter to somebody just like that, they might forget about it or maybe lose it somewhere on the way.

The only sound I could hear as I climbed down the stairs was the rustling of wings. Like when a bird, surprised to find its cage door open after a long time, stands there hesitantly, not believing that all it needs to do is spread open its wings and fly away.

ACKNOWLEDGEMENTS

I WANT to thank my dear friend Želimir Periš for his suggestions and constructive criticism during the initial phase of this novel. Thank you to Veronika Santo for reading its final version. Special thanks go to Srđan Damjanović, without whose generous help in creating a credible setting for Instantly, I think that the novel would look quite different. And lastly, my family. Thank you for your patience during those times when I isolated myself and was absent, when I could belong only to myself.